PATRICIA LINCOLN

WestBow Press®
A DIVISION OF THOMAS NELSON
& ZONDERVAN

Copyright © 2018 Patricia Lincoln.

Cover Art and Interior Image Credit: Paula Giltner

All rights reserved. No part of this book may be used or reproduced by any means, graphic, electronic, or mechanical, including photocopying, recording, taping or by any information storage retrieval system without the written permission of the author except in the case of brief quotations embodied in critical articles and reviews.

WestBow Press books may be ordered through booksellers or by contacting:

WestBow Press
A Division of Thomas Nelson & Zondervan
1663 Liberty Drive
Bloomington, IN 47403
www.westbowpress.com
1 (866) 928-1240

Because of the dynamic nature of the Internet, any web addresses or links contained in this book may have changed since publication and may no longer be valid. The views expressed in this work are solely those of the author and do not necessarily reflect the views of the publisher, and the publisher hereby disclaims any responsibility for them.

This is a work of fiction. All of the characters, names, incidents, organizations, and dialogue in this novel are either the products of the author's imagination or are used fictitiously.

Any people depicted in stock imagery provided by Getty Images are models, and such images are being used for illustrative purposes only. Certain stock imagery © Getty Images.

THE HOLY BIBLE, NEW INTERNATIONAL VERSION®, NIV® Copyright © 1973, 1978, 1984, 2011 by Biblica, Inc.® Used by permission. All rights reserved worldwide.

ISBN: 978-1-9736-4352-4 (sc)
ISBN: 978-1-9736-4353-1 (hc)
ISBN: 978-1-9736-4351-7 (e)

Library of Congress Control Number: 2018912712

Print information available on the last page.

WestBow Press rev. date: 11/09/2018

To Roy,

who was the rest of me,

the best of me.

Foreword

I am especially grateful to Stephen Gillmore, my 'technical advisor' and friend, without whom this little book would never have made its way into print. It has been an honor to work with WestBow Press and a challenge to meet their high standards of Christian integrity in the writing of the story.

Christian literature must lead the way in reaching out to the hurting, the traumatized, the broken. We live in a broken world – Christians, too. Life happens – to Christians, too. And we must not play the ostrich and stick our heads in the sand about these things that matter. In our piety, do we presume that Christians do not suffer? Do we *dare* to pretend that they never doubt or question or lash out at God or lose control? It *is* possible to write about the "deep valley" issues without being sordid or graphic. That is what I have attempted to do. Yes, life happens. But grace abounds as well.

Patricia Lincoln

Chapter One

"All right, now ladies. One more time. This dinner and evening will be flawless -- if I have to *hurt* somebody to achieve it. That's **hurt** – as in *maim* or *murder*. Do we understand each other?" Taylor Harlow stood with one hand on a hip, surveying the dining room of the apartment with the critical eye of a Master Sergeant at inspection.

Both room-mates nodded affirmatively – Amber with a wiggle of her shoulders and a teasing look in her eyes, Anne with a tolerant side-smile as she folded the last napkin.

"Amber, telling you not to flirt with Matthew is like telling the sun not to rise in the east. But, I've already warned him about you.

"And Anne, you may *not* skip out on this party. I need your help. I want everything perfect and you're a good organizer."

"All right, of course. I just don't want to be in the way," Anne said.

"You? In the way? Annie, darling, I love you dearly, but you must know that you give off *non-entity* vibes when you meet new people, so I'm not worried about you flirting. In fact, Matthew and I will be so preoccupied, he'll probably barely notice you're here. He is very focused when he's trying to finalize a project."

"I consider myself thoroughly analyzed and soundly put in my place," Anne replied, grinning.

No three young women could have been more different – in personality, and consequently, in looks, mannerisms and interests.

Taylor Harlow, an architectural/design assistant in the fourth-generation, family firm, **The Breckenridge Corporation,** was tall, slender, with enhanced black hair perfectly groomed in a short, below-the-ears cut. She considered herself on the way up and not to be denied. She wore dark business suits, ivory silk blouses, black kid leather heals and – thanks to the flower shop on the first floor of their office building – *always* a rosebud (fresh, not fake) in her lapel. Glenn Hurley's book, *People of Power,* was her bible.

Taylor Harlow had her cap set for Matthew Stuart Breckenridge IV, which was no secret – to him or to anyone else.

Amber Cleary had a head of gorgeous, thick, auburn hair that flowed around her shoulders and around her neck as she moved. She reminded one of a television shampoo commercial, constantly swinging her head and running her fingers through her hair. It was her crowning glory and she maximized it. Amber moonlighted as a photographer's assistant in order to pay the bills while she waited for serious work in the theater. She was an accomplished pianist and her musicianship had developed into an able, on-the-spot entertainer at cocktail parties and 'coming-out' receptions – however, *coming out of what* was a bit dubious. Amber did not play well enough to provide any sort of bankable income. At the studio, however, she had learned the importance of a striking first impression, the ready smile and coloration in personal appearance. She generally wore pinks, soft shades of green and lots of turquoise jewelry. In her dramatic life, she was eager to respond to any appreciative young man who was willing.

Anne Whitfield, Taylor's cousin, on the other hand appeared, as Taylor reminded her, more of a non-entity – almost apologetic about being in the way of the other two women – like she was interfering in their life-style just by her presence. She wore her ripe-wheat golden hair almost shoulder length. On this night, it was in a loose French roll with a wisp or two escaping around her ears. She wore a mocha brown, suede skirt cut right at the knees because *"that's what knees are for, to mark skirt length"*. A soft pink, long-sleeve, tailored blouse and a wide dark brown leather belt with a brass buckle and a necklace of three tiny gold chains completed the ensemble.

Matthew Breckenridge, thirty-three years old and a YALE graduate, was VERY good looking, but honestly did not seem to notice – or care. He was serious minded, but smiled easily – and Oh, that smile! He was currently shaking up the Breckenridge firm with new innovations in design, especially with absurd ideas about solar energy.

With Taylor's help, Matt was finalizing drawings and specs for a round, totally solar-powered home so well designed that there are no provisions whatever for auxiliary heat. Thus, they needed some place away from the office to finalize sketches and details without Grandad 'B' looking over their shoulders decrying the utter waste of time, ink and energy on such impossible frivolity. Taylor had suggested they have a working dinner at her apartment and intended for it to be a very, very special experience.

In true designer fashion, Taylor left no detail ignored. Fresh flowers on the table as well as the coffee table and a window seat or two – heady, spice scented oil in the bottom of each arrangement. Dinner would be catered in, but all indications that it was not home-cooked dispensed with before Matt's arrival. Cooking and homemaking were not of particular interest to Ms. Harlow, but Matthew need not know that at this point. *"By the time he is mine, it won't matter."*

Maplegrove was one of several smaller suburbs scattered around the edges of the city, each one with its own promoted unique features. This one had been incorporated and developed around a grove of old-growth maple trees which became its namesake and its center of activities. As much as is still possible for up-scale, contemporaries to socialize as a community, Maplegrove did its neighboring at the grove. Summer lawn-chair Pop concerts, 4th of July political rallies and pet shows, children's Halloween costume parades, January ice sculpture contests and the annual Fall Festival of the Arts. Everybody participated and picnicked.

Directly across the street from the east entrance to the grove stood 'The Breckenridge', a five-story, modern apartment complex – an imposing example of the newest and best architectural design from THE BRECKENRIDGE CORPORATION.

When Matt arrived, Taylor introduced Amber -- quickly so as not to give her time to 'present charms' -- and then, turning to Anne, said, "Matthew, (she called him his full name because Granddad Breckenridge felt it was important for the company image and it was important that she humor the old man) this is my cousin, Margaret Anne Whitfield. She is staying with us for a short time this fall, while taking post-graduate classes at the University."

Anne's handshake was forthright, firm but gentle. She looked directly at him with a twinkle of mischief and said "Why, Taylor, he seems much nicer than you said!"

There is a sudden and windy intake of breath from Taylor. "Anne! I never – I uh, - I didn't say" – she blubbered.

Matt laughed happily and, nodding slightly, said, "And a good evening to you, too."

Anne smiled, "It's a pleasure – and please forgive me. I couldn't resist. I don't get one up on Taylor very often."

Throughout the meal, Taylor tried to keep the conversation on the office – projects, budgets, people she and Matt knew, but the others did not. (This was their exclusive territory and she subtly kept Matt's attention from wandering adrift.)

Amber flounced and preened and successfully managed to disrupt the trend of thought but had very little of constructive interest to add. Her subconscious objective was to attract attention. She needed to be noticed – she did not know *how* to be *unnoticed*.

Anne had been quiet throughout be meal but, during an oh-so-brief lull, asked Matt, "The names Matthew Stuart Breckenridge obviously had special meaning within your family as well as the corporation. How did that come about?"

He laughed heartedly. "It's really quite amusing how it 'came about' as you say. Are you sure you want to hear it?"

"Absolutely," she responded. She pushed her plate back and, placing both arms on the table, leaned forward. Taylor looked directly at Anne and raised her eyebrows questioningly. Anne didn't catch the subtle reprimand.

"Well," he started, "the story is told that the original Matthew Stuart Breckenridge was almost named Matthew Benedict Breckenridge.

"It seems that three generations ago, the proud father announced that his just-born boy child should be called Mathew Benedict Breckenridge, being old patriarchal names from somewhere in the family history. The new mother, my great-grandmother, however, with much consternation, forcefully but effectively skewered the suggestion of Benedict.

"Hear me now, my lord and master," she facetiously interjected. "I participated (rather painfully, I might add) in producing this baby boy and *my* name will be attached prominently. 'Matthew' I know, 'Benedict' is unknown to me, 'Stuart' was my name before I married, and 'Stuart' it will be."

"So - - the surname remained and the paternal history went the way of all suggestions made by vulnerable new fathers, weakened and humbled by the birth of a first-born son - - - - or at least, so I'm told."

Anne chuckled at his supposition.

Amber sat restlessly throughout the telling, idly brushing phantom crumbs from her skirt, crossing and re-crossing her shapely legs – but Taylor paid rapt attention. Her antenna was up toward any information concerning the Breckenridge family that might someday prove valuable.

"So", she said, as she casually straightened his dessert fork beside his plate, "when you have a son, will you continue the tradition?"

He smiled slightly and answered vaguely. "Who knows what the future holds, right?" But in the process, she had diverted the conversation once again and she began to discuss his father's involvement in the company and how soon he projected it would be before he, himself, was made Chairman of the Board.

When it was obvious *this* subject was going nowhere, Taylor changed tactics. "Matthew, we really must get busy on our project."

Anne got up first and hovered briefly over the table. "Let me clear this while you finish your coffee. You can spread your paperwork out on this table. There's plenty of room and the light will be perfect."

As she picked up his plate, he turned to her and asked, "So, do you go by Margaret Anne, or Margaret or Anne?"

"Mostly Anne," she replied. "My daddy used to call me Annie. My mother called me Margaret. My brother called me Maggie and," shrugging her shoulders and grinning, "I suspect my kids at school call me all sorts of strange things."

Taylor added dismissively, "Anne is a third-grade teacher and actually believes the little wretches have a possibility of becoming useful citizens."

Anne smiled. "Yes, when I'm not playing at being a college student, I teach. I took a leave of absence to pick up a couple expanded courses in teaching troubled children and new approaches to Mathematics."

Amber jumped in with both feet. "Personally, I never did care for ANY math, new or old. Who cares how many miles a train will go if it's travelling at 50 miles an hour and if the wind is blowing behind it or toward it? All I need to know is what the numbers on the clock mean and what the amount in my bank account is." And with that bit of wisdom, she floated off to her own diversions elsewhere.

Everyone pretty much ignored her.

Matt, to Anne, "Why *Third* Grade?"

"It's a good age. They're old enough to be eager and quick learners and young enough to be at least moderately innocent – in fact, the different sexes can't stand each other at that point." With that, she carried dishes into the kitchen and left them to their project.

A bit later, a restless Amber sat down at her grand piano in the living room and began to play softly. This winsome young lady was not rigidly technical in her playing, but her romantic nature and sense of drama made her interpretation of most semi-classical music outstanding and she played with great feeling.

After Anne finished in the kitchen, she brought fresh cups and a coffee pot to the dining room table, then took a cup in to Amber who was beginning to play Debussy's "Claire De Lune". Anne set the coffee down on a table nearby and quietly picked up the violin lying there. She tucked it under her chin and began to follow the piano phrasing with a very pensive, reflective, single-tone counter melody.

In the dining room, Matt stopped -- mid-sentence and mid-motion. He was mesmerized -- and totally unprepared for the feeling of emotion which nearly overpowered him. The hair on his arms almost tingled. Those clear, sweet string tones -- it was breathtaking. Taylor, sensing his mood, stopped talking and covered his hand on the worksheet with her own, trying to be included in his moment and thankful for an opportunity to touch.

The masterpiece ended on a high, well-drawn note, fading into a long distance of purified air. Anne carefully laid the violin back in its case, paused to give Amber a little hug, kissed the top of her head, and said to her, "You are truly a lovely blessing." Then she stepped quietly though the French doors onto the patio where evening was just beginning its own melody of repose.

No word was spoken, but Matt turned and looked questioningly at Taylor. She shrugged, unimpressed, and said, "That's just like her. Now she'll go sit for a while in what she calls her *sunset chair*." She rolled her eyes, shook her head and bent again over the world with which she was so familiar and into which she knew no one else could intrude.

"Oh, come quick. Come look at this!" Anne exclaimed excitedly from the French doors to the patio.

Taylor, disturbed yet again, glanced at Matt. "It's another sunset. You'd think the sun never sets in anyone else's world but hers. Go look if you want to – I'll sit this one out."

As soon as Amber saw that Matt was going and Taylor was not, she jumped up and, taking hold of his arm, crowded herself out the door beside him.

Matt stood with his feet wide apart and his arms crossed over his chest. "Wow."

"Yes, Wow!" Anne breathed. "It's a gorgeous gift, direct from the God in Heaven Himself."

They watched in awe as the colors faded, brightened and rearranged themselves in an ever-changing spectacle. Without saying a word and without taking his eyes off the miracle of color, Matt quietly eased into the other chair, reluctant to break the spell. A cool breeze flitted across their faces, as in quiet benediction.

After a very few minutes, Amber broke the moment. "Oh, let's do go in. There's a chill of dampness in the air – I can feel it, can't you?"

Matt left a long, thoughtful look in the direction of the glorious spectacle on the horizon, then reluctantly turned toward the house and back to duty and diligence. However, Matthew Stuart Breckenridge IV felt disturbingly unsettled and distracted.

Chapter Two

Two evenings later, the girls were at supper – *supper* this time, not *dinner*. In fact, it was vegetable soup made from leftovers from the famous evening a couple nights before.

Anne's phone rang. She answered. An unfamiliar female voice inquired, "Anne Whitfield?"

"Yes, this is she."

"Would you hold please for Matt Breckenridge?"

"Yes. No. Wait -- just a minute. Are you sure he is calling Anne Whitfield?"

"Yes ma'am. Would you please hold?"

"Certainly."

Matt's voice, "Is this Margaret Anne Whitfield? Annie, Maggie, and who knows what else?"

With her trademark amused chuckle and crooked smile, Anne answered. "Yes sir. All of the above at your service."

"Well, I'm glad for that because I am desperately in need of help. I need an expert in Child Development to accompany me to my niece's second grade science fair at six thirty Friday night."

"Oh, I'm sorry. But, you see, my expertise is in *third* grade."

"Second, third, ninth. You don't understand. She is making her *exhibit* and wants me to demonstrate how the sun warms the earth -- and I'm afraid I'm in over my head. I need some supervision here."

"I was led to believe, sir, that solar energy was one of your specialties."

"Oh yes, ma'am. I know the subject matter, but I don't speak "second grade". Besides, I promised to take her for fries and a milk shake afterwards. I might be begging here, but will you come with me?"

Silence – Full of expectancy on his part and hesitancy on hers.

Finally, "Yes. Certainly. I'll be happy to come. Tell *your niece* not to worry about a thing."

The next day in class, during an *exhilarating* lecture on "The Natural Tendencies of the Troubled Child", Anne received a silent text.

"How do you talk to kids?"

She shot back, "Like anybody else, except with enthusiasm. In class now. Call after 1:00."

Her phone rang at 1:02.

Matthew fretted, "They're going to think I'm an old fuddy-duddy."

"Of course, they're not. Your niece knows you already, right? She doesn't think you're an old fuddy-duddy. She obviously loves you – or at least *likes* you -- and wants to show off you and all your great wisdom."

After a moment, she said, "Tell you what. If we can go about thirty minutes early, I'll bring a couple props that will help you. And the kids will love you. I promise."

"Yes. Yes! OK! I'll pick you up at 6:00 sharp. Got to go. Thank you, thank you."

The look on Matt's face was beyond description when he pulled up in front of THE BRECK that evening in his Corvette (fortunately a convertible). Anne was sitting on the curb dressed in khaki jeans, a crisp long-sleeved white shirt with the cuffs rolled back -- as in 'ready for work' -- and a dark brown, suede vest. She was wearing brown 'walkabouts'. Beside her sat a rocking chair, a three-foot tall plastic rubber-tree plant and a shopping bag with LET'S PRETEND COSTUME RENTALS printed in bold letters on the side.

He took one look at her accumulated props and bemoaned dramatically, "I knew this night would be a disaster. You didn't specify a moving van."

"Not to worry, my neurotic friend," Anne consoled. "I've seen stranger looking outfits than this on old 'Beverly Hillbillies' re-runs." She handed him a couple tie-downs. "You stow the rocking chair. I'll straddle the plant so it won't blow out." And, away they went with Matt behind his Blue-Rays, hoping to be incognito.

When they got to the school, Anne, being completely familiar with the normal lay-out and hierarchy of a school, asked the door greeter for an empty room. Once unloaded and inside, she opened the rental bag and directed Matt, "Take off your belt."

His eyes popped open, he feigned shocked surprise. "I beg your pardon, ma'am?"

She laughed. "You're perfectly safe, sir. There are children about."

He complied. She rolled it up, dropped it in the bag and handed him a pair of bright yellow suspenders, a fake white beard, a pair of gold-rim eye glasses with the lenses removed, and a can of body powder.

She helped him fasten the suspenders and hung the beard over his ears. Then, approaching him with the talcum powder and grinning, she said, "The only thing about this is that you're going to smell like lavender sachet." And she began sprinkling white powder into his thick, black hair.

"Does the scent of lavender render a man weak and helpless?" Matt asked.

"Absolutely not. It just speaks of a 'free spirit'. Besides, you're an old man. An old fuddy-duddy, remember?"

"Of course. I forgot . . . . momentarily."

"Now," she handed him the glasses. "Put these on and the image is complete."

He complied and experimented looking through them. She reached up and pulled them down on his nose about half way.

"You need to be authentic. Sometimes you look through them and sometimes you look over them. Got it?" He practiced – quite well, actually. Sometime during this back-stage dress rehearsal Cassandra, the instigator of all this madness, popped into the room. She looked at her uncle with surprise, then realization, then awe. Then, with little girl delight she burst into a fit of giggles.

She ran to him, knocking the glasses completely off, and squealed, "Oh, Uncle Matt. I love you!"

Amused, Anne raised her brows at him, saying without words, *See, I told you so.*

"You'll sit in the rocker to talk to them, but when you enter -- can you walk like a very, very old man?"

"Of course. We watch Grandad B. often enough, don't we, Wee-one?" He winked at Cassey. She giggled and darted from the room. "Even in my nightmares – uh, my dreams," he corrected.

Anne ignored the hint of sarcasm in the private family joke and said, "Now, Uncle Fuddy-Duddy, here are your props. The light bulb on the cord is for making sunshine with heat, the plant is for making shade and all the other stuff goes without explanation. As you so succinctly reminded me earlier, you know your subject. So from here on it's 'Improvise and ad lib.'

"And away they went toward the gym, the science fair, the second-grade booth and infamy. Matt assumed the walk and posture that had been assigned as they made their way, for two reasons. He needed the practice *and* he didn't want anyone to recognize him. However, the effort was fruitless because the moment his niece saw him, she jumped up and down, excited, and clapped her hands delightedly – which, of course, attracted all sorts of attention. He looked pleadingly at Anne. She shrugged her shoulders, gave him a thumbs-up and stepped back into the crowd. Obviously, *she* was not to be counted on for any more help here at all, he thought.

While Matt waited for Cassey to tell the observers what her display was about, he had time to scan her booth – his 'execution chamber' for the next hour and a half. Unknown to him, she had painted a back-drop for her booth. It was childish and very crude, but *almost* everything was identifiable and, actually, a pretty accurate depiction of solar heat at work.

It contained a blue sky, a huge yellow sun with rays beaming in all directions, and a large green tree on one side with plushy green shade underneath. In her imaginative way, when a ray from the sun hit the ground, she had painted it with squiggly lines which turned and went back up into the air. A red flower in the front corner had little arms and hands reaching up toward the sun.

A house, of doubtful sturdiness, in the background had a large black square in the middle of the roof and he noted that the sun's rays hit that spot and went right through the roof and into the house. Interestingly, a scruffy brown dog was lying in the foreground and for whatever purpose seemed to be dozing in the sun – except that it was wearing oversized sun glasses. Beside it stood a bottle clearly marked SUNTAN LOSHUN. Other dubious objects portrayed were also labelled – such as HOWS and SUN PANNOLS.

For some reason, Matt had a flash of inspiration. Wouldn't it be a hoot to have the whole thing framed and hung on the wall in the front lobby of The Breckenridge Corporation? He had paid big bucks for less appealing art.

Cassey stepped in front of him and announced in her most professional stage voice, "This is my Uncle Matt. He is Mr. Uncle Fuddy-Duddy." And the torture began.

The fact is, it was repeated **four times** throughout the next 90 minutes. Did these kids *never* get tired and go home?

Matt had called for back-up transportation for the theatrical excess loot, boot and bounty and eons later, he and his two women were holding down a booth at Ricky's Burger Spot. Cassey had shared two large orders of fries with her uncle but had refused to allow two straws in her chocolate shake.

She hugged him twice and told him "This was the best Science Fair I've ever had!" No one mentioned the fact that it was only the second one in her entire life.

But now her little head was lying on her folded arms on the table edge and her eyes kept trying unsuccessfully to stay open.

Anne said quietly, "Technically, it's none of my business, but why were you the sole representative of her family for this activity?"

"I'm not surprised you asked. Her parents, my brother and sister-in-law, are on an architectural dig in the Middle East somewhere. They enjoy digging up what someone like me struggled to build millenniums ago. As to the rest of the family, that is a lo-n-n-n-g-g, uninteresting story. But," he looked down at Cassey, "the twerp here and I just happen to be best buddies."

There was a soft moment as both adults watched the sleeping child and mused their own private thoughts.

Anne broke the silence, "You accomplished more than you intended, my friend. You not only had their rapt attention and taught them about solar heat, but you taught them another valuable lesson."

"What was that?" he asked.

"You taught them that *old* people know things, too, and that *old* people can be fun and lovable."

"Lovable. Is that what I was? I thought it was called *foolish*."

She paused purposely for effect, then added, "No, you won't

feel foolish until your picture comes out in the People Section of the *Daily Sun* tomorrow morning. That was a reporter taking those pictures, you know."

"Oh, Dear Lord." Matt groaned.

She laughed heartily. "The Lord had nothing to do with it. He gave you the ability and the nerve and then He turned you loose to have some fun with a bunch of His favorite people. Even though you couldn't call Him by name, you gave Him credit when you said, 'The creator knew what He was doing when He gave us the sun to heat the earth and all the other good things it does for us.'"

"I *was* pushing it a little there, wasn't I? How do you know who the photographer was?"

"Because he was pumping me for information. He wanted something 'scoopy', I think."

"The family name will be *besmirched* forever! What did you tell him?"

She grinned. "I have no idea who that man is," I told him. "I never saw him before in my life."

Chapter Three

A storm broke inside the apartment the moment Taylor walked in the next evening slamming doors and tossing things. The words *cloudy, dark, threat of lightning and damaging winds – take cover immediately* came to mind.

"Well, I hope you're satisfied, Miss Meddlesome!" Taylor barked ferociously. "You've succeeded in making Matthew Breckenridge the laughable object of the entire office. No one would have known it was him except for Jack Mason's by-line and the accompanying picture."

"I expect everyone was laughing *with* him and not *at him*," Anne replied. "Did the story happen to mention that the second-grade booth on solar energy was the highlight of the Science Fair and won 1st prize?"

"Yes, but that's not the point! Matthew Stuart Breckenridge has a professional image to maintain and light bulbs and rubber tree plants certainly do NOT lend themselves to the respect that he and I are endeavoring to secure for our new solar energy project. Grandad 'B' was the only one who seemed to enjoy that Matt's 'Mickey Mouse' presentation had proven his *own* point very effectively."

"Taylor, I'm sorry that you're so offended. But Matt did call me and ask for my help, you remember."

"Oh, so it's Matt now, is it?"

Anne, facetiously, "I'm sorry. I should have said, Mr. Breckenridge in deference to his professional image."

"Yes – and you should have said 'No' when he first called about that little kid's juvenile science project. You don't need to be a 'buttinski' every time someone yells for help."

"That little kid is his niece and she idolizes him. Since much of his family seems pretty critical of him, I'm sure it's refreshing to him to have one of them actually *like* him."

Taylor threw her best punch. "You know what? You think just because you mothered three younger siblings that makes you an expert on all family relationships. Well, here's a news bulletin! Your years at home with those kids deprived you of learning even the most elementary social graces."

Anne looked down and seemed to be absorbing the verbal condescension. Finally, she raised misty eyes and looked at her cousin.

"I clumsily mothered *and* fathered those three little ones from adolescence into adulthood and in the process, I learned more about grace than anything else could have taught me. Perhaps not *social* graces, but grace in its truest form – direct from my – and their – loving Heavenly Father. And, though you don't agree, that's all I need to know on the subject of grace."

She added, "It seems that I am causing you much unhappiness, so I will gracefully return to my non-entity status and cause you no more grief. I'm truly sorry, Taylor. Please forgive me. OK?"

Taylor snipped, "All right! Let's *say* no more about it – but be assured, I won't *forget* about it soon."

As Anne headed for her futon, she said, "Good night, Taylor. I appreciate you letting me stay here."

If Monday evening had seemed an uncomfortable scene in the apartment, it was an anti-climax to Tuesday's homecoming for Taylor. She sensed something amiss when she let herself in the door about 7:00. No supper smells, no relaxing music playing – just whimpering sounds from Amber at the piano, accompanied by some sort of *dirge* in blues rhythm. (Amber was profoundly capable of integrating her many moods into her music.)

The luggage rack in the back hall was gone as were Anne's two suitcases. Upon inspection, her section of the hall closet was empty and her green towels gone from the bathroom. Her violin was not on the back of the piano.

"Amber, where is Anne? What's going on here? And, for pity's sake, what's the matter with you?"

Amber sobbed. "Nothing – I don't know – and everything – in that order."

Taylor seated herself on the end of the piano bench and put her arm around Amber. "OK, now, baby girl. Tell me whatever you *do* know."

Amber leaned her head into Taylor's neck and sobbed. "I don't know anything except Anne is gone! I mean *gone*, gone. She left me a note, but it doesn't tell me anything."

"Let me see it, dear." A small, scented but tearfully soggy note was thrust into her hand.

Dear, dear Amber,

I have enjoyed you so much. You are so beautiful and you have taught me that beauty comes in many forms. . .your sweet smile, your spontaneity. . .and your lovely music is the most beautiful I have ever experienced.

Thank you for letting me share your life for a brief moment.

Yours in Christ,
Anne

"Was she gone when you got home?" Taylor asked.

"Yes, yes, yes. I didn't even get to hug her goodbye. Do you think she'll be back?"

"No. Not Anne. She's not hasty in making decisions, but she's deliberate."

Taylor moved toward her bedroom, pulling off her jacket and kicking off her shoes. She was completely non-plussed. "Why would Anne do this to me?"

And then she saw it. Another small envelope propped against the pillows. Slowly she sat. *Slowly*, she picked up the note. *Slowly*, she held it to her face and inhaled the familiar scent. *Hesitantly*, she slipped her thumb under the flap and, with trepidation, began to read.

Dear Taylor,

Ever since you and I played on Grandmother's swing when we were five years old, I have looked up to you and wanted to be just like you. I childishly prayed for black hair just like you and for your cute little ears. I was jealous of your shiny, black Mary Janes. Remember those? I even wanted to have the Chicken Pox when you did!

All through grade school and into high school, I idolized you – the parts you played in drama club and even when I missed out on cheerleading with you because Coach Dennis said I didn't have your vitality and verve. Remember Coach's love for that word? Everybody had to have <u>verve</u>!

Recently, when you were gracious – there's that word again – enough to welcome me into your home, I have felt nothing but honored. But now, I feel shame. I am so sorry that I have caused you to be disappointed in me.

Dear Taylor, please believe that it has been mere ignorance on my part. I would not, for anything in all the world -- except, of course, my Lord -- hurt you.

I have located a room and have secured a couple tutoring jobs, so I can give you back your space and I will not meddle and muddle your plans for a professional career.

My prayer for you is that the success you long for is that which matters most in this life and the next. Please read Jesus' words in Matthew 6:19-21.

Yours, as always, in Him,
Your Annie

Taylor slowly folded the letter, silently creasing and re-creasing the folds between her thumb and forefinger. She stared, but did not see. She wasn't angry because she knew Anne never said anything insincerely.

"Annie may be naïve, but she *is* truthful," she said to herself.

Chapter Four

A week later –

The presentation on "Harnessing Solar Energy" by The Breckenridge Corporation team at the national conclave was a huge success. The model and demo of a circular, rotating 100% solar-powered private home was virtually expanded into potential commercial applications on a wall-sized projection screen. The firm and its two star presenters were lauded and applauded. Other design/engineering groups signed consulting contracts and project oversight agreements. Even two competitors wanted in on the action. Fortunately, Taylor, with the help of their legal department, had insisted on all the necessary licensing, copyrighting and patents before going public.

As Matt told one of his contemporaries, "That lady does not trust anyone. She would copyright her bedtime prayer, 'Now I lay me down to sleep' if she had thought of it first."

In the company jet on the way home, Matt suddenly said, "I can't wait to tell your cousin. She'll be proud of us, but especially you! I can sense that she is your most loyal fan. Let's call ahead and make arrangements to take her to dinner tonight to celebrate."

Taylor was silent.

"What? Too tired? Not a good idea? Why?"

The proverbial 'pregnant silence' ensued.

Matt looked at Taylor and raised his eyebrows in question.

"Because I don't know where she is," she said.

He gestured with an upturned hand and more eye language, waiting for more.

She rolled her eyes, "Oh, all right. So, we had a discussion after the 'Uncle Fuddy' debacle - - - and she moved."

"Moved? As in moved OUT?"

"Yes. Yes. Yes. She moved out!"

"Where to?" Why?"

"As to where – I have no idea. As to why – you see if you can guess."

She reached into her purse and handed him her letter. "Here, read for yourself. Then just leave it alone. I'm tired of it."

Matt silently read Anne's letter. He let it slip into his lap and leaned his head back with his eyes closed.

Taylor stared out the plane window and then quietly began. "Annie has always been my supporter and anchor – an ever-ready leg up or pat on the back. When we were little, I would swing, she would push me. I got in trouble, she cried. In high school, I made 100's and A's, she made 99's. I often suspected, on purpose.

"When her parents were killed, she more or less deserted me and I resented that. I knew she was busy with those younger kids and I often felt sorry for her, but our lives had taken different paths. I missed her, sure, but I was 'on my way' to bigger and better and never looked back.

"Now, after all these years, she shows up again in my life – right now when I'm at a professional pinnacle. And, unassuming as she is, I absolutely cannot have her 'commonness' hold me back. I'm a leader. Truth be known – she's an *also-ran*."

Matt, sat with his eyes still closed, listening to this diatribe, his heart breaking. He did not know how to react.

He did not feel anger. No – he understood Taylor well enough.

He thought, *"She actually feels like Anne has been a hindrance to her. She does not feel any remorse about her own actions. Dear God, she's feeling no responsibility whatever."*

As the plane touched down and amid the bustle of finding briefcases, gathering 'stuff' and setting feet to solid ground, there was time only for brief "Goodbyes" and "See ya's".

Taylor, in her fatigue, pretty much dismissed the conversation and was merely looking forward to a long, relaxing soak in a hot, foamy bath.

Matt, on the other hand, had already settled a rather detailed plan for tomorrow in his mind. At home, he stripped, showered, fell into bed and slept like a hibernating bear.

The next day, as Anne exited Grant Hall after the conclusion of class, Matt was sitting on a bench balancing a brown paper sack and two large Styrofoam cups.

He spoke. "In today's world, it's very difficult for a person to completely lose one's self," he said.

"Uncle! How nice to see you! So – are you trying to lose yourself?"

"Don't I wish!" he replied. "But I've decided that's what *you* have in mind."

She smiled her little sideways smile and sat down. "Not *mis*place. Just *dis*place."

Matt commented, "Taylor and I have been in New York all week, so I had no idea about your little 'dust up' until on the flight home, yesterday."

Anne looked around quickly, "Oh, is she with you?"

There was a moment's pause. She glanced at him questioningly. Their eyes locked.

"No, of course she's not. I'm not here to hurt you, Anne." His dark eyes continued to hold her gaze. She looked away without a word.

Suddenly, Matt slapped his leg. "So! I brought lunch." He reached into the bag and pulled out two wrapped sandwiches. "Smoked turkey – or smoked turkey?"

She grinned. "I think I'll go with the smoked turkey." Glancing pointedly at the drinks, "And a cold drink, please."

He held them up. "Cherry limeade - - - - or cherry limeade?"

As they ate, "So, why the clandestine move?" he asked.

"Several reasons, really. I wanted Taylor to be able to truthfully say, 'I don't know *where* she's living.' I didn't think it mattered where. I was, after all, trying to get out of her way. And, as for you, I had absolutely no idea *you* might need to know where I was. Besides - - -". Suddenly she stopped. "Why am I telling you all this?"

"Because I asked – and because I *do* need to know where you are."

Quietly, "Oh."

By this time, the after-class crowd had cleared and the two of them, shoulder to shoulder, ate their sandwiches and drank in not only their limeades, but the sights and sounds of a lovely late summer day. Quiet communication without the burden of conversation.

Time went by – as did a butterfly or two.

Matt gathered up the wrappers and cups. He stood and looked down at Anne.

"Let's go to dinner tonight at *Lost Pines*. No Cassey – no French fries – no curfew. Seven o'clock?"

"No fries? Sounds lovely. Let's do!"

He turned a 180 and disappeared around the privet hedge.

Chapter Five

When Vincent, a long-time waiter at Lost Pines saw one of his favorite diners arrive, he gave a nod to the Maître D' which said "He's mine, please". His boss nodded back and led the couple to Matt's table by the window.

Anne had never been here before, but was enthralled – more with the view, really, than the restaurant itself. Looking out at the pine forest and the naturalized plantings, she said, "Who needs to eat? The scenery is enough to fill any appetite."

"Yours, maybe, but not mine. My soul says, enjoy. My stomach says, eat. What are you hungry for?"

"Oh, please order for me. I can't read half the words and might order Poached Hippo in Hollandaise -- or something."

When Vincent appeared, Matt introduced Anne. "Vincent, this is Anne Whitfield, teacher, student, advisor and special friend. She plays tricks on unsuspecting new acquaintances, so watch out!"

After the waiter was gone, Matt took her hand and bowed his head to pray. No "Do you mind?" No "May I?" No "Shall we?" He just prayed quietly. Conversation at the tables around them became more subdued during his prayer, but if anyone was uncomfortable, he did not notice. He praised God for the beauty of the scene out the window, he expressed thanks for His love and care and he asked for blessing on the food.

Anne leaned back, crossed her legs and her arms. "Now, tell me about the trip. Was it a success? Did you accomplish what you hoped for?"

"A totally uneventful trip. The crew was on time, the weather held, and we didn't run out of gas or peanuts. That's a good trip." Then he told her briefly about their well-received presentation and said, "Yes, we came away with a briefcase full of enthusiastic solar converts."

One distinct advantage of Anne's having moved on her own was that Taylor was not aware that Matt and Anne were out together at least once a week.

Sometimes a Saturday afternoon bike ride, sometimes horse-backing at a near-by stable, always dinner together afterwards and often Wednesday night prayer time at her church. They did not attend the same church, so their Sunday morning worship was not together.

The bond between them grew stronger. They never tired of visiting and listening to each other. After that first long evening at Lost Pines it became their favorite refuge from outside pressures and distractions. Vincent 'mother-henned' them atrociously. Matt spoiled *him* equally.

The solar project and its ensuing involvements monopolized most of Matt's and Taylor's interest at work – so much so that a complete, new department (space *and* personnel) was assigned to it. Taylor was often beside herself with supervision and could not understand how he could just walk out some evenings, claiming he had other plans.

Matt, though not entirely blind to her maneuvering, did not fully realize the *intensity of her intent* and was oblivious to most of her advances and innuendos. But he was *not* a block of wood. He fully realized that she was determinedly possessive of his time and interest.

He always dreaded taking Anne back to her tiny 'bed, bath and hot plate' room after they had been somewhere. But she was not in the least apologetic about her accommodations – in fact, she seemed so grateful for the blessing of it she often thanked her Father for it when they prayed together. Besides, he realized Anne had a certain pleasure in being able to make it on her own and he saw how important it was for her to be self-sufficient, relying on no one but God.

After their third dinner out, he held her hand as they walked to her door. She was laughing heartily at something *stupid* he had said and had unconsciously brushed her head against his shoulder.

A sudden feeling of intense emotion swept over him like an electric impulse. He stopped them in their tracks and turned her toward him. His other hand went up and brushed that wisp of hair back behind her ear. With his fingertips, he tenderly traced her jawline and lifted her chin.

Looking deep into her eyes, he whispered, "Stop smiling, Ms. Whitfield, because I'm going to kiss you."

His lips touched hers in the sweetest, gentlest expression of tenderness known to lovers anywhere.

When he withdrew, he kept his curved forefinger under her chin and continued to look into her eyes.

"It just occurred to me," he said, "that I am hopelessly in love with you."

She trembled ever so slightly and whispered back, "This won't do at all, sir."

But neither of them moved. He kissed her again. She nearly fainted.

He held her other hand firmly between them to steady her.

"And why not?" he asked.

"Because you're spoken for."

"I was not aware of that."

"Oh," she breathed.

He cupped her chin with both hands and gently melted her heart again with his lips.

With her eyes still closed, she said, "Will you go home now, before I pass out?"

"My darling, I will step off the edge of the *earth* if you tell me to," he said.

"No, just go home - - - -so I can think."

He held her by both shoulders and asked, "Are you all right?"

"I am delirious," she replied.

She made a 180 and disappeared inside her door.

The huge bouquet of roses, delivered to her small apartment, reminded her of the teachers' lounge at school. Someone always had a birthday, anniversary or argument at home – so floral arrangements constantly adorned the snack table waiting to be hauled home to loving arms.

The card read, "To help you think."

Chapter Six

The B's, as they were known in the company, were in Palm Springs for a couple weeks and this seemed like a good time for Matt to take Anne to his home. Knowing her, he felt that a gradual introduction into his world would be less frightening. He knew she would eventually absorb the rigid social structure graciously as she did everything else. But he wanted her to feel at ease about it. He dreamed of the day when she would color it with her own artistry and add her own warmth and charm.

He walked her through the house and introduced her to the staff who were present. He especially enjoyed the way she and Ardyth, his old nurse bonded.

Ardyth gave Anne a warm, welcome hug and said over her shoulder to Matt, "Have you confessed your many infractions to the *rules of the manse* or am I going to invite this young lady to lunch with me one day?"

"She is strictly off-limits to you, my dear lady", he replied. "I'll thank you to keep your stories to yourself. I will tell her what I want her to know *when* she needs to know it, thank you."

As she walked away, the nurse winked at Anne and said, "We'll talk later."

They sat on the overstuffed lawn furniture under a shady pergola to visit and enjoy a light lunch of cold sandwiches and mugs of hot soup. Not once did Anne feel even a twinge of guilt about not being gainfully employed in studying one of her college courses.

Matt leaned back, thoughtfully massaging the sides of his tea glass. "You have been around Taylor enough recently that you must be fairly familiar with the inner workings of our day-in-day-out endeavors. My life is a very public and involved one and leaves very little room for personal activity. So -- there's really not much for me to tell."

Then he added, "But your life at home is much more individualized and varied. Tell me all about Anne Whitfield's Life on the Farm chapter by chapter, verse by verse."

He put his feet up on the lounge and settled in. Anne pulled her feet up under her and sipped her tea. *Where does one begin when your life has been so full? How much is too much?*

"Next to Christ Himself, my kids have been my life – by choice, rather than by force. The authorities encouraged me to send them to foster homes when the folks died, but I wouldn't hear of it. I was stubborn enough and just barely old enough to make it stick." She smiled and paused a moment.

"You would really like Andrew. He is nothing like you – and a lot like you. He's smart and ambitious and *very* capable.

"Like I told you before, all three of them went to college - on scholarships and part- time jobs and Ramen noodles.

"But Andrew fell in love and married the second year. He was determined to quit after that year. So he borrowed $10,000 from his new father-in-law, bought himself a beat-up old pickup and some yard mowing equipment and started his own landscaping business.

He was already well-known as a go-getter, is strong as an ox and loves people. He has made it big time. He now owns three trucks, has two full-time employees and his wife does their bookkeeping."

"Do they have children?"

"No, not yet. These days that's a matter of choice. I'm very proud of him."

"As well you should be. So – what about the twins?"

"Ah, yes, the twins." A twinkle of a smile. A slow drink of tea. A swat at a fly.

"For the first time in their lives, they could not agree on something. It was about which college to attend. I hated to see them separated, but our minister, who knows them as well as anyone, suggested maybe it would be good for them. He thought it might be easier now than if and when they marry. So – off they went – a little timorously, I thought, but bravely.

"However, for the first couple of months I think they remained joined at the ear, to paraphrase an expression. They bought themselves new phones with some of their scholarship funds, calling them school supplies.

"Nathan is studying Computer Science, of course, – what else? Julia is going to save the world with Environmental Studies.

"Oh, my!" she added as an afterthought. "Parenting ain't for the weak-willed and faint-hearted. It takes G-U-T-Z!"

They laughed.

Matt stood up and took her hand, leading her toward the wooded area behind the patio.

He said, "Let's walk, but please don't stop talking. I love the story and I love to hear you tell it." After a few minutes, with nothing more forthcoming, he encouraged her, "Did you make part of your living from your farm?"

"Oh, yes. We have been thankful to have it. It's a lot of work, but I love the natural beauty and the serenity and the freedom of that way of life." *I can't wait to get back to it.* she thought.

However, Matt immediately noticed a flicker of change in her voice. He put his arm around her shoulders as they walked. "Does Andrew see to the farm while you're gone?"

"Not all of it. He doesn't have time. I have rented the house – hoping and praying that it's not completely trashed. Andrew is taking care of the premises and I have share-cropped the land. Andrew's wife, Becca, is temporarily paying the bills and collecting the rent for me."

"What kind of crops do you raise?"

"Wheat, corn, milo, soybeans, in various combinations. I'm old-fashioned, I guess. Many of today's farmers double-crop the land, meaning they grow an early crop and then a late one on the same field. Which also means they only farm about the top six inches of the soil and have to use lots of fertilizer and chemicals to keep it all going. I like to turn the soil over deep, raise one crop and then let it rest and rebuild 'til next season. My farmer agrees, but it's getting harder and harder to find one who does."

Matt shook his head. "I feel like an ignorant city bumpkin – if there is such a thing. How do you *know* all these things?"

Anne chuckled, "I guess I know a little bit about a lot of things, but not enough about one thing to be an expert at anything."

Matt turned to her and raised his eyebrows. "How's that again?"

She bumped him off the path. "You heard me and you know what I mean. Life teaches you what you need to know and I thank God every day. He has been my teacher and protector. I've been really scared a lot of times, but He's always shown me something to nudge me along or make me laugh."

They sat on an old log beside the path and Matt could stand it no longer. "Annie, will you love me?"

She looked down at her hands folded in her lap. She took a long, shuddering breath and looked up at him and said, "I have absolutely nothing else to give you – but I will give you my *heart* and I will love you forever and even beyond."

He swallowed her with his arms and she raised her head to him and gave herself completely to his kiss of promise.

Chapter Seven

Anne was going to the Breckenridge home for dinner.

The invitation had been extended reluctantly by Claire and arbitrarily by Breck. It was encouraged by Matt and accepted warily and hesitantly by Anne.

The table was purposely set as extravagantly as possible but our *lady of the hour* was cagey enough to watch her *prince charming* and pick up the appropriate fork at the proper time and wise enough to remain ignorant of innuendo. The folks were extremely cordial, but there was tension. No one was fooled -- everyone realized there was 'class action' going on there.

Later that evening when they were alone, Claire could stand it no longer. She exclaimed, "Oh, Breck, what are we going to do? This just must not happen! Whatever is Matthew thinking?"

Breck replied, "I'm afraid it's too late, Claire. The man is already completely gone. I'm sure you recognized all the signs."

"Surely we can *try* to discourage him!"

"If we try and it doesn't work – what then? If we build a wall, we could lose a son."

They sat brooding for a while. Then Breck said, "Tell you what. I'll talk to Matt tomorrow while everything is still on all our minds.

I'm sure the young lady sensed a bit of reticence on our part. But I will not be caustic or demanding. I don't want to drive a wedge between my son and myself and I *won't* make a threat I'm not willing to carry out."

Claire asked, "Anne seems like a smart young woman and might be aware that her station in life could be a hindrance to Matt's position in the company and community, don't you think?"

"I sincerely hope so, darling."

Late the next morning, at the office, Mr. B. emailed his son. *Lunch at the club? Two o'clock. I'll drive.*

Within those eight words were questions and innuendos that Matt could only imagine. His dad never had lunch with him unless he was promoting an idea. Two o'clock meant that Dad wanted very few people around to witness and/or hear their conversation. The curtness of the invitation meant there was no refusal. Asking by email meant he wanted no questions asked beforehand. And the immediacy, after yesterday's family dinner, meant that it all came down to Anne.

He emailed back. *Fine. I'll be ready. A*nd he meant that in more ways than one.

After they were settled into a secluded corner Matt said, "Dad do you realize this is the first time since I've been back at the company we've had lunch together for a reason other than business?" He paused and reflected, "In a way, it's as much my fault as yours. I never invited you, either."

He gazed out the window at something a million miles away. And, still staring, he quietly said, "I wonder why."

The moment broke. He looked back at this father. "I suspect this *is* about business, isn't it? You and Mom don't list Anne Whitfield on the asset side of the ledger for the future of the B Corp, do you?"

"That's a bit too succinct, perhaps, but – no, Son, we don't.

Anne is a lovely young woman and we both admire her a great deal. But, Matthew, she is not right for you – and like it or not, you *are* the future of the B Corp." After a long, tense pause, he continued, "I cannot state this more emphatically. You *must not* pursue this relationship!"

Matt leaned forward and put his elbows on the table. He looked squarely in his dad's eyes and spoke softly. "Ever since I have been a 'consenting adult' I have discussed this whole marriage thing with my *Heavenly* Father." He accented the word 'heavenly' – and then he grinned and said, "I guess that's been almost half my life, hasn't it?

"Anyway, it hasn't been a big issue with me, but I earnestly promised the Lord I would wait to marry until I knew, without doubt, that He was in it. Dad, He has given this marriage His blessing. I'm praying now that my *earthly* father will, too."

He leaned back in his chair in a more relaxed position but did not relinquish the floor.

"The B Corp is rock solid, thanks to you and your father before you. I feel like you have the same confidence in me or you would not have been grooming me all this time to carry on. We both know that this institution will not crumble if its junior executive ruffles the waters a bit. I pledge to you here and now that I will do my best to make you proud of me. But – Dad – my *best* will be enhanced by the love and loyalty of my best friend and bride-to-be, my Annie.

"Furthermore – and this is not a threat, it is a testimony – I would abdicate the corporate throne and give up everything Breckenridge, past and future, if it should come between my love and me."

Breck was almost in shock as he continued to look at his son. Gradually, his eyes began to glisten -- then he smiled ruefully. He looked down, rearranged his silverware, then looked back up at Matt and said, "Are you going to eat that last roll?"

"Break it in half and let's share it," Matt answered.

Chapter Eight

As would be expected, the time eventually came when Taylor Harlow and Anne Whitfield must come to terms with the serious issues involved.

Anne was determined to mend fences with her cousin – a *lifetime* of family fences too valuable to be allowed to crumble and disintegrate. Taylor would have it be known that she did not need any further contact with the nemesis of her past life. But Anne did not believe that. She knew 'Ms. Independent' too well. She could read her eyes when they chanced to meet. She knew Taylor was hurting and needed resolution as much as she herself did.

She called Taylor and asked her to go to dinner.

"All right. But it'll need to be Tuesday night. I'm really, really busy catching up with Matthew's work. He's been somewhat preoccupied lately. Tell me your address and I'll pick you up. Let's go to one of your little supper spots where you'll be comfortable and I can come directly from work."

Anne agreed, the innuendos notwithstanding.

After heated and fruitless discussion over spaghetti and salads, it was obvious to Anne that no forgiveness would be forthcoming, and to Taylor that the unexpected romance was set in concrete. She was crushed. She felt defeated, jealous and uncontrollably angry, demonstrated by much car-door slamming and tire squealing out of the parking garage.

Finally, concerned, Anne said, "Honey, you're upset. Would you like me to drive?"

Taylor looked at her like she had lost her mind.

"*Honey?* You dare to call me *Honey?* And you **dare** suggest I would let you drive my car? How could you? Why **would** you? Isn't it bad enough that I have to take you home at all?"

"All right. All right. But at least take the River Road, away from all the traffic. And I don't care if it *is* your car. Please have the decency to hold your cigarette out your window. The atmosphere is bad enough in here without having to smell your smoke, too."

"So, now you're going to criticize the very air I breathe?" Taylor yelled.

Anne refused to let her emotions get the best of her. She answered quietly, "No, Just the air *I* breathe. And for goodness' sake – slow down for that next curve. You know this road as well as - - - -"

The curve. The speed. The one-hand on the wheel. The distraction. A split second – and an eternity in time.

There was a horrific screaming of brakes. The car rolled completely over two – maybe three – times and came to rest on the driver's side in the edge of the river. Both women were knocked unconscious. Moments passed, airborne tires continued to spin.

When Anne revived – how long had it been – she was completely disoriented with the car upside down and backwards. Finally, she managed to get out from behind her airbag and release her seatbelt. Her chest and lower stomach hurt something fierce, but she could move so she reasoned nothing was broken.

She looked over at Taylor who was still unconscious – or – "Oh, no. Oh God, no!"

Taylor's head was completely submerged under the water pouring into her open window. Anne crawled to her and tried to lift her head out of the water but couldn't get it high enough. She searched frantically for *something* to prop it up, grabbed *somebody's* purse and tried to push it under her head. But it was too tight -- the seatbelt held her too tight!

She yelled at Taylor, "Taylor, wake up!" No response. She yelled at God, "God help me!" Suddenly, she remembered her phone in her pocket – and called 911.

For the eternity it took for help to arrive and knowing full well it was too late, Anne continued holding Taylor's head as high as she could to her own chest and sobbed her heart out.

Chapter Nine

Dr. Ted Milton had practiced a good part of his ER training on Matt and his brother as they crashed through adolescence. Broken limbs – *tree* limbs and *boy* limbs – seemed to be their specialty, but there were also a noticeable number of football and horse-racing catastrophes. He was also a dear family friend and Matt called him Uncle Ted.

"Anne is banged up and severely bruised which will take some time to heal on its own, but listen good, son. That is not her most serious injury."

Matt was shocked. "What do you mean? Is she going to be all right?"

"Of course, she is. But she has suffered a post traumatic breakdown." Matt sank into a chair. Dr. Ted continued, I use the word 'breakdown' because I'm old and I get sick of the word 'syndrome'. *Besides* this is more sudden and complete than any mere syndrome. *Another besides*, being old, I don't always buy into the most recent experimental treatments. And, *besides*, I know you both, I love you both and I believe in you both."

"Thank you, dear friend. How can you diagnose all this so quickly?"

"Because I know trauma. And this young woman is suffering.

We're taking care of her nerves for the time being – but that can't continue for long. At present, she is out of control. She is crying, trembling and constantly moaning, "It's my fault! I killed her! Why Taylor and not me?" And a lot of other things I know nothing about." He paused and sized up Matt's reaction.

Matt looked away from the doctor's eyes and covered his mouth with his fingers. He *would not* get emotional. He *would not* fall apart. He looked back at his Uncle Ted and said merely "Talk to me."

"From what you've told me, I sense that her siblings could offer moral support, but not the hard, practical help she needs in this extreme. I also know you are passionately and permanently in love with her. She needs you now, Matthew, and only you can help her climb out of this dark hole. My question to you is, "Would you be willing to make the sacrifice of time and profession? Can you make a tremendous personal sacrifice to care for her 24/7 without attempting to satisfy your own physical needs?"

"Of course, of course. But I don't know how!"

"Take her away from here for two or three weeks – whatever it takes for her to forgive herself and look to the future again."

Matthew shook his head. "She wouldn't go – because of the morality of the thing."

"So -- marry her."

"What?" Matt almost shouted.

"Marry her! Now. I know you're planning to soon anyway. Tomorrow will give you time enough to throw off your harness. I want to keep her overnight. You can do your proposing and convincing here. We can do the blood work and you're both over 21 so there's no three-day wait on the license."

"Uncle Ted, you're a genius! But you can bet, Miss Margaret Anne Whitfield is going to throw a fit!"

"As for you, young man, you sold the whole city of New York on crazy, rotating round houses. You can surely convince one sick little girl to go away with you. And as for Anne, you are going to see that right now, she doesn't really care about *anything*. She is living below the surface of life. She's afraid you think the accident was her fault and so she's reaching out to the only one who still loves her, Jesus. It will be up to you to start from there and bring her back into the realm of your love.

"Besides, if you can pull this off, Claire will probably be beside herself with glee. The last time your dad and I played golf, he said she is finally convinced there is no stopping you – she's only concerned about Anne's family 'clodding' up the whole affair. I believe that's the way she phrased it. So, you and the Lord take the lady and make her well."

The two men shook hands, then looked at each other and grabbed each other firmly in a bear hug. They held for a long time, time in which much respect and affection and trust was unspoken.

When Matt first entered Anne's room, he was shocked. The only visible sign of her was a long lump in the bed that looked like a body had already deceased and been covered. Except that the lump was shaking and whimpering. He walked to the side of the bed, coughing lightly so as not to startle her.

"Is Margaret Anne Whitfield under there?" And quoting from the first time they met, "Is this 'Annie, Maggie, and who knows what else?"

One hand moved and grasped the edge of the sheet, used it to wipe both eyes – and then a red, swollen, barely recognizable face appeared.

"You have the wrong room." And turning her head away from him, "Go away."

Thus began a very long, tortured conversation, gradually – oh so gradually – turning to the proposition at hand.

Anne was completely subdued and repressed. She had already decided that she was guilty of great, unjustifiable harm, so what else mattered?

He summarized the whole thing for her, "Legally, we will be married, but emotionally, mentally and physically, I will wait for my darling to come to me."

She smiled, wryly, "That shouldn't be too difficult for you. I certainly don't feel or look very appealing at the present. I must say, you show great courage. I am so afraid, but you must know – if you asked me to sky-dive without a parachute right now, I would welcome the opportunity."

He dared not let his shock show at hearing such bleak words, so he said brightly, "Sorry. No sky-diving on this trip. In fact, we won't be flying – we'll drive. The Vette will be our chariot to great adventure!"

Anne sighed and tried to look excited though she couldn't feel it – even remotely. Eventually, she relented to his bizarre proposal.

That very evening, Matt sent a long letter to Andrew and both twins, briefly explaining the plan. For obvious reasons, he did not give an address where they could be reached – they all had his phone number. He had already called them after the accident, assuring them she was not seriously hurt and had been in touch with them by phone several times.

He passed along the doctor's diagnosis, assuring them Anne's condition was not serious physically, but she was suffering acute mental and emotional trauma. He relayed Dr. Ted's orders, but kept the tone of the letters as light as possible.

He signed them, "Please pray for us. Yours and His."

As a P.S. on Andrew's, Matt added, "I had intended all along to ask your permission to marry your beloved sister, but this crucial time crunch prevented that. We both feel it is necessary to make our time together legal – but, most importantly, to honor what we believe is God's will."

In Matt's true matter-of-fact-style, he closed with "Thank you for understanding." He thought, *I have no idea if he understands or not. I'm not entirely sure I understand.*

Matt hit the license bureau at 9:00 the next morning. Anne's hospital dismissal was scheduled for10:00 – more or less – hospital time. By 11:14, they were on their way to the hospital chapel.

When they walked in, Anne's pastor, Matt's brother, Mark, and Amber Cleary were standing just inside the door grinning from ear to ear. This was a case where the *party* almost preceded the wedding.

Amber could not contain herself and saw no need to. "Darlin', if I couldn't have him, I'm just glad I can witness his getting locked up by my best friend!"

Mark grabbed Matt's arm and said, "I've got your backside, brother – here and at work. I told them not to look for you until they heard you roar into the garage."

Naturally, there were major adjustments and re-arranging at The Breckenridge Corporation with Taylor's sudden death and Matthew's sudden abdication.

All patents, copyrights, pro-formas and contracts, technical and electronic, had been tightly sewed up early in the project. There were two newly licensed architects who were full of 'spizz' and eager to jump in at a moment's notice. Breck, himself, though not excited about the concept, was astute enough to know its future. He took the responsibility of holding the longe line on the fresh, untrained stock. Besides, Claire had headed for places across oceans where she could be incognito and saved from further embarrassment.

Chapter Ten

Matt let Anne sleep undisturbed – except for food – the whole first day. He busied himself, electronically, with the office, cancelling appointments, temporarily re-assigning some of his projects, writing absentee letters, and sending up-date notes to family and close friends. Starting the second day, he insisted she accompany him everywhere he went. "You don't have to participate or pretend to enjoy yourself. You don't even have to smile. You just have to keep me company. You already know I'm not a loner – I'm a people person."

"You're a good people, too, Charlie Brown."

For five days, they went to the park with box lunches, and took long top-down drives through the countryside. One day they went to the zoo and sat a long time watching the Panda, Ming Loo, with her new baby. Another day, they visited an Amish community, where they bought hot loaves of fresh bread and freshly churned butter and homemade apple-butter. Then they sat in their car and ate most of it while watching little barely-clad Amish boys swing on a rope out over the creek and splash into the water. At first, Anne shuddered visibly at the sight of the water. Matt acted like he didn't notice. He smiled and said "Those boys are having such silly fun. I'll bet they're about second or third graders.

"And we know about second and third graders, don't we? I mean, hey, I've spent three hours with a brutal gang of seconds and survived to tell about it."

"So, *tell* me," she asked. "What was the scariest part – what was the sweetest part – and what was the exact moment when you realized, 'I'm actually having a good time?'"

He smiled reflectively and began to describe the experience, but very soon his listener had dropped off in peaceful, sunny slumber.

He looked at her and whispered to himself, "Don't fret, Matthew, my man. You can save all those memories for another time – like boring your grandchildren with them in your 'rocking chair-chamomile tea' days."

Matt checked in with Uncle Ted every day and called or e-mailed Andrew every other. Ted Milton gave invaluable advice and encouragement – and praise for the progress. Andrew apparently admired Matt's patience and fortitude. Throughout the three weeks, he showed in several ways, that he had become very proud of his new brother-in-law.

Sometime during the second week, Matt dared to say, "Amber called me today."

"How is she?"

"She's O.K. Hurting, of course. She's found a smaller apartment she can manage on her own – not at THE BRECK, of course. She misses you. She said you always kept everything calm and pleasant around the house. Her words, "Anne is my best friend, maybe my only *real* friend."

After a moment or so, Anne commented, "I didn't realize that until the wedding."

Matt changed the subject, "Do you know what I'd like for my next birthday?"

"Whoa. Do you always make a birthday wish-list ahead of time?"

"Not since I was sixteen. But believe me I did when I was a kid. Always worked, too. But quit distracting me. I'd like you and Amber to play a private concert for me. You need to know country western is my favorite music when I'm down and feeling sorry for myself. I can tolerate small bites of classical. Jazz just goes on and on. But whatever you call the kind you played the night we met reached me through and through. That's what I want!"

Anne looked thoughtful. "I don't remember what it was but, be assured, your slightest wish is my command and a duet you shall have. The sorry situation here, though, is that I don't know when your birthday is."

He feigned shock. "It was on the license application. Dear madam, are you in the habit of signing a document you have not read thoroughly – especially one that enslaves you for the rest of your natural life? We really must talk more about this at a later date."

———

A day or two later – with no warning, Anne said, "I believe Taylor probably *loved* me – out of a sense of duty – but I doubt she ever *liked* me."

They were having lunch and she had not eaten more than a few bites before she pushed her plate back.

"What makes you think that?" he asked.

Looking down, she reflected, "One time, when I was thoroughly discouraged with one of my classes, I lamented to her that it was hard moving to the other side of the school desk again. I was just trying to make fun of my own misery. She scoffed at my attempt and almost yelled, 'Oh, don't pretend to be all that depressed! You, with your faux humility! You're not humble, dear cousin. You're completely self-satisfied!'

"But then she said to me, 'You had plenty opportunities to raise yourself above your family's *rustic* ways if you had been willing to pay the price!'"

Anne looked up. "Those words punched holes in my heart."

He didn't rush her. It was subtle, but very clear, that she needed to remember and find resolution. She needed to let go of someone who was already gone – by whatever path she chose to take.

"I had no idea she was actually ashamed of the 'rustic' side of the family." Ann reflected.

She added, "Maybe we were *rustic*. Maybe that's why I always felt I could not keep up with her. Maybe that's why she nicknamed me her 'Tag-along'."

He gave her more unbroken moments. Then he covered her hand with his and said quietly, "Maybe she didn't know *how* to love. Love does not acknowledge rustic or sophisticated. Love is a four-letter word, Anne – and so is *give* and *care* and *kind*. But so is *hate* and *mean* and *hurt*. A person does not learn those things overnight, darling. They take practice."

Anne acknowledged that premise, before saying, "Taylor loved you, you know."

"No, she loved the *idea* of me," he said. "The *Breckenridge* idea, the adornment idea, the ownership-of-the-company idea. Taylor was driven by her dreams."

He added, "Taylor died the way she lived – in dramatic black and white. She wanted it all – and actually gained little of real worth. If something or someone was hers, she notched her gun and looked around for a new target. If not, she set her sights and took aim.

"But, those are only outward signs of her character. We cannot know what her true heart felt – but we *do* know what *your* heart has felt for *her* -- all your life and now in her death. You have loved her and love her still."

Ann looked at him with a long, thoughtful expression. She understood what he was saying, but she was obviously reflecting upon something else, too.

At last she said, "A couple weeks ago, Taylor called me twice one evening. But . . ." She looked down and shook her head, remembering. "When I saw who was calling, I didn't pick up." She looked up at him with pain in her eyes. "I thought I didn't want to listen to another diatribe about how thoughtless and selfish I was.

"Oh, Matt. What if she wanted to apologize? What if she felt remorse and wanted to talk? What if she just wanted to talk? Like we used to when we were kids? Under the bed covers with a flashlight. . . with cracker crumbs everywhere . . . trying to see who would fall asleep first . . ." Anne hugged her knees to her chin.

Matt listened, groaning inside with the desire to gather her in his arms and slay the dragons she was fighting. He did not '*fuel the fire*'. He listened – with his *heart* as well as his *ears* – and he prayed.

"Annie, you have been fighting a frightening, solitary battle and I can only imagine how lonely you must have felt at times. But now, sweet soldier, your Lord is reaching out to take you by the hand and move on with you – the two of you together."

Long moments passed.

"And you, too?" she asked.

"And me, too."

One day on the golf course during the second week of Matthew's absence from work, Breck asked his good friend, Ted Milton, "What on earth is going on with my son and his sudden bride these last couple weeks? He has shared very little with me and *nothing* with his mother, but he said he is following your advice and that he has your blessing."

Dr. Ted replied, "You know I can't discuss it with you. Suffice it to say your son is doing a very difficult and courageous thing. Don't discount him. Pray for him. Now, are we going to play golf or flap our jaws?"

On an evening when the sunset over the lake promised to be spectacular, our hero – business exec turned care-giver – announced, "Tonight is L.O. night. We clean out the frig and use everything in it to make something worthwhile. Our entertainment for the evening hovers just above the horizon and is free. So – I'm taking orders."

He swished open the refrigerator door and stood back.

Anne looked inside, opened a couple drawers, rearranged some plastic cartons on the shelves and said dubiously, "I'll have the Chef-iest Chef Salad you can make."

"Chef-iest? Woman, what on earth does that mean?"

"That means *very little salad and all the 'stuff' the chef can find to put on it.* But, kind sir, can we have some peanut-butter toast to go with it? And maybe a good, big, cup of hot coffee?"

Matt made the salads while Anne made the coffee and rigged up TV trays beside the outdoor lounge chairs. She was determined to be relaxed and not 'heavy up' the atmosphere of this gorgeous evening.

However, when they prayed *after* the meal – as they often did – she broke. Tears ran down her cheeks. "Why? Why? she cried. "I would have been ready for death – but Taylor was not! And her death was probably my fault!"

"Tell me the reasons why you think that," he said quietly.

"I made her angry in the first place . . . .and I knew better. I knew from when we were kids how out-of-control she could get. I insulted her when I suggested I drive. I was the one who suggested going on the River Road -- I should have realized how dangerous it is in places. I told her to roll down her window because of the cigarette smoke. If the window had not been down, perhaps the water would not have come in so fast. I got disoriented and couldn't find the seatbelt fast enough. I couldn't hold her head high enough, long enough. I . . . I couldn't . . . I didn't . . . Matt, it was my fault!"

"Annie, there is no consolation for your loss, except in any happy memories you can conjure up from childhood with Taylor. But there *is* consolation for the distress of your perceived responsibility.

"You know and I know -- and God Himself knows -- that you wanted only the best for your cousin. You *did not* do any of those things to hurt her. Truth be known, you were trying your best to protect her from herself. The whole point of that entire evening was an effort on your part to restore a relationship."

He stood up, looked at her tentatively, pushed both hands deep into his pockets and began to pace. The only sound for several minutes was a mocking bird, doing his comic best to fill the air with something cheerful.

Matt turned toward her and said, "OK. Let's pretend for a few moments that all those things you are worrying about were true and that you did them with evil, ulterior motives. Do you really think the Lord could not forgive you? Is there some scripture – any scripture – which is His word on the subject – where He says He cannot forgive you?

"Still assuming all that were true, what would be the only criteria here? Being sorry and truly repentant. Think of Peter – Peter's repentance and God's forgiveness made Peter a bigger man and stronger Christian for the rest of his life. If God forgave Peter, if God could forgive you, could you not do the same – forgive yourself?

"This is a time when the mind has to give direction to the heart. Your heart is breaking, but your mind knows undeniably what the truth is. Let your intellect reason this thing out and encourage your heart."

He sat down beside her again, close and strong. He winked and said, "Sorry. When I preach, I pace. But the sermon is free."

She looked at him with a smiley face and teary eyes. *Oh, she loved him so.*

They were quiet for a long time, watching the sun dip into the horizon. The golden sunset seemed to portray a *putting to sleep* – at least for this day – of the pain and guilt.

Anne reached for Matt's hand and said, "As the psalmist says, 'Be at rest once more, O my soul, for the Lord has been good to you.'"

Matt prayed, "Dear Father, thank you for the blessing of nature's beauty – always, every day – but especially this beautiful, peaceful sunset. Thank you for Anne and all she means to me.

"Father, help her to deal with the loss of her family member and friend as just *that* and not as a personal failure. Please send your spirit to give her peace. Give her 'Simon Peterness' to do great things for you. In Jesus' precious name. Amen"

After a minute, "Peterness?" she asked.

After another minute, "Yeah."

Chapter Eleven

The paradox of Anne's healing showed itself in her lingering question *Why not me?* rather than the question which usually surfaces in times of trouble, *Why me?*

She did not question the accident which brought on all this trauma. Instead, she questioned – in fact *wished* – that *she* could have been the one who did not survive.

She tried to explain it to Matt. "Taylor was always *almost* angry, like she was fighting some unseen enemy. She was always reaching, pushing -- never satisfied, never enough. She couldn't seem to find happiness, whatever the circumstances."

"Happiness is always a by-product of some other effort." he said. "If we seek it directly, we always miss it. Taylor thought it came from accomplishments, accumulating things and fame.

"I think the inner anger came because she really knew better. She had been brought up the same way you were. She had learned early in life what really matters. If she was fighting some enemy, it was herself. That's what made her angry."

Anne cried, "If only she could have lived long enough to make peace with herself and The Lord."

Matt sat on the floor in front of her with his arms folded across his knees "Listen to this." He quoted from the 23rd Psalm, "He prepares a table before me in the presence of my enemies.

"We have been talking about Taylor's possible enemies. Let's think a minute. We all have enemies. Right now, you are struggling with one -- a feeling of regret that has you in its clutches.

"Annie, the idea of refreshment served in the presence of enemies is a fascinating symbol. It means we don't have to have all the problems solved before we can find nourishment for our souls. We can find happiness even if there are events in the past that would come back and haunt us if they could. Life is filled with enemies, but we can live good, happy lives even in their presence."

She eagerly responded, "Oh, yes. That's so wise. I want to think about that some more. Thank you, thank you for those thoughts. You always seem to know how to clear my head."

"I admit," he said, "not all my *preaching* is original. One of my favorite authors is Don Ian Smith. He was a rancher and found life lessons in so much of creation. I have all his books. They are great stabilizers to me when I think my world is about to implode.

"He lived the kind of life I have dreamed of since cub scouts camp. Except for his being a preacher. That's not for this bloke, I assure you."

Anne smiled, "There's more than one way to spread God's love and good news. Don Smith had his way – you have yours."

"I hope so."

The metamorphosis of his butterfly occurred a moment at a time.

In her waking hours, judgment and reason gradually began to shepherd her emotions, to lead her from "the valley of death to still waters".

But the nightmares. Oh, the nightmares! The sudden sense of rolling – over and over. The screaming sounds of collapsing metal and rushing water. Water everywhere. Taylor's panicked, staring eyes just below the surface of the water. The sudden heat and cold sweat, the claustrophobic horror of being unable to breathe.

The fatigue of stress begged for sleep, but the dread of unbidden flashbacks denied her that healing, restorative balm.

She and Matt both knew their foreseeable future, though exciting, would be shadowed by occasional psychological bumps and bruises.

One night Matt got up to get a drink and found Anne sitting on the sofa with her head against the back. Her eyes were closed but tears streamed down her face. He sat silently beside her. She opened her eyes, but did not move.

He put his arm around her shoulders and drew her close to him. With the thumb of his other hand, he wiped tears from her cheek and touched them to his own face. Silently, he spoke a thousand words with that one gesture.

Matt spent as much as an hour in his room early each morning, searching for appropriate words from the Lord in scripture and strengthening thoughts from other writers he admired. They had, from the second day, settled in for prayer and devotion before bed.

Though Anne was attentive the first few nights, she did not audibly participate, but he pilgrimed on. One night, she said to him, "Say that last verse again. What a lovely thought. I want to take that to sleep with me."

A few nights later, she spontaneously began to pray – a prayer of gratitude for a multitude of blessings. What utter joy Matt felt. He held her hands while she prayed and leaned his forehead into hers. His tears dropped onto their clasped hands. That was the first time he spoke about the *real* reason they were on this 'sabbatical', but he felt so compelled, "I see you from afar, my darling. And you are on your way home. Thank you, Father."

As providence and the God Almighty would have it, eventually Anne picked up her violin and slowly began to express long-repressed emotions which needed to be *felt* out loud. At first, her music was reflective, but broken, as though she could not follow a phrase through to its conclusion – occasionally ending on a dissonant tone.

One afternoon Matt sat on the floor with his computer on the coffee table, answering some office emails when, from outside somewhere, he heard beautiful strains of violin, "I was weak, but now am strong. . .Just a closer walk with Thee." Slowly, piteously sad. Then – a pick-up in tempo – her foot tapping a little bit of rhythm. "Let it be, Dear Lord, let it be."

Matt jumped up, bumping table, computer and Coke out of the way. He stood in the door and looked at her. She glanced at him and smiled. He returned a wide smile, winked at her, folded his hands in mock prayer and bowed low to the ground.

She turned her back to him, pretending to ignore him, and continued playing. He went back to clean up the spilled Coke.

Tuesday night of the third week, Matt chose the book of Ruth for their Bible reading. He prayed earnestly for guidance and asked God to make him half the man Boaz was. Anne, again prayed for peace and joy and thanked God for Matt, boasting that he was *already* the man Boaz had been.

When he came to kiss her goodnight, she was remembering some craziness that had happened that day and they both got tickled, both adding their own versions of the incident. As usual, it got sillier in their-telling.

Matt laid down beside her, leaned on one elbow, and looked at her. "I love to see you smile", he said – then *purposely* eased the moment by adding, "except for that piece of spinach on your tooth." And the famous crooked smile finally came out of hiding.

"Humph." She hopped up and went to slosh the spinach away.

They laid on their backs beside each other for several minutes, longing to be one, but neither willing to make the first move. This time, it was *she* who was hungry – for his touch and his affirmation that he found her desirable. It was *he* who was afraid – that he would frighten his precious kitten back into hiding.

After a few moments, Anne raised her arm and laid it across the top of his pillow. She touched the shock of black hair above his forehead and slowly began stroking it with her fingers.

"*Oh God,*" he prayed silently. "*Help me.*"

"I love you," she whispered.

He turned his head toward her and softly asked, "Forever?"

"*Beyond* forever."

He raised up and took her in his arms. Slowly, gently, hungrily, with almost unbearable patience they became one.

As he softly held her head against his chest, he whispered, "Welcome home, my darling. I, too, will love you -- forever and beyond."

Chapter Twelve

At *barely* first light the next morning, Anne was awakened by the smell of coffee. As she opened her eyes, Matt leaned over her with a cup in one hand and waved a piece of stale cinnamon roll under her nose with the other. She turned her head away in disgust.

"Yuk."

He popped it into his own mouth and handed her the coffee. "Mrs. Breckenridge, since you so irresponsibly ran off and got married without any planning or fore-thought, it is my duty to inform you that you have the very devil to pay for such thoughtlessness. And he is presently nipping at your heels.

"You – the party of the first part -- have two days to confer with your affianced – the party of the second part – as to a workable plan for your immediate future and to implement whatever negotiations necessary for peaceful co-existence with said second party." He gasped in a huge breath and sat down beside her.

Her mouth opened wide. "You've been up for hours, preparing that speech, haven't you?" She tilted her head and scowled up at him. "May I point out to said bossy party of the second part that I was under duress and was unfairly influenced when such infraction occurred. I therefore claim innocence."

"Be that as it may – there is much to be done. Behold! I have heretofore prepared a worksheet (he whipped a rolled-up piece of brown grocery bag out of his hip pocket) labelled 'Non-negotiables' and 'Options' – with a subsection entitled 'Pros & Cons'. It would seem that the first order of business to be discussed is *Where Are We Going to Live?*'.

"He glanced at her – which was a big mistake. He looked at her again with the mussed up hair and the dancing eyes. He tossed the paper on the floor, took her coffee away from her, pulled back the covers and slid in.

Later – quite a *bit* later – she leaned up on one elbow and 'zipped' the forefinger of her other hand down his chest.

"You are unzipped," she teased.

"I am *completely* undone, my dear," he responded.

"You'll need to put on your worksheet – whenever you find it – that I already have an apartment. You can list that under 'Non-negotiables'. OK?"

Matt roared with laughter. "Ah, hah! By the time I move in with you, bag and baggage, electronics and sound system, golf paraphernalia – and two Great Danes – you'll beg to move that item into 'Negotiable'".

On that note, they showered, dressed and headed to the kitchen for bacon and eggs. Thus began a full day of planning, emailing, phoning and yes, negotiating.

They decided that Anne would give her thirty-day notice on her little apartment and use it, in the meantime for a 'landing spot' when needed.

She was already under contract for the next school term at Spring Valley so that was a given. In fact, she would need to leave for home in three weeks.

Matt would leave most of his stuff – including the non-existent

Great Danes – at home and would bring two bags to the apartment. Then he would check out possibilities for a proper apartment in one of the Breck Buildings.

Anne would give thirty-day notice to the renters on the farm. She would live there during this school year and make plans for refurbishing it into a week-end retreat and country home in the future.

In the back of their minds were variations of: *How are we ever going to stand this arrangement and being apart so much? Hey, we have both endured worse in order to achieve a life-time of <u>never</u> being apart again."* Then, finally, *"We can do this."*

They agreed on two major, immediate goals. Number one (and top priority) they would spend a day at the farm before going back to the city. They would invite Andrew and the twins to meet them there for an uninterrupted, face-to-face time of getting acquainted, debriefing and re-assurance that all is well. They desperately needed that, especially Anne.

Number two, Matt's personal goal was to use this intervening time to somehow encourage an understanding and relationship between the two women he loved. He also intended to concentrate on bringing his mother, Claire, back on board the family ship. His dad did not seem as concerned about the *mutiny* as Matt, but for himself, he longed for her enthusiastic support of Anne. He smiled to himself. *If nine months was long enough to grow and give birth to a healthy baby – another human being – surely the nine-month school term would be time enough to germinate the seeds of a lasting friendship between his mother and his wife.*

Matthew loaded bags and baggage into the car and came back for Anne and the last small items, including the now vitally important work-in-progress, "The Plan". She stood in the door and turned around one last time, slowly surveying the room.

"It's crazy," she said. "This place seems like a sort of refuge – and, yet, in a way, I can't wait to get away from here."

He just laid his hand gently at her waist and waited. After a brief moment, she turned and walked to the car. He closed the door and followed her.

Chapter Thirteen

Without having seen the farm house, Matt agreed to Anne's first idea.

"Non-negotiable is extra bedrooms -- because Mark's family will love to visit often. And Amber will always be welcome".

Matt eagerly jumped in. "And Cassey must have a pony -- and a puppy -- and maybe a tree-house?"

"Whoa, back!" Anne burst forth. "Ponies and puppies need a lot of daily care and attention. That plan needs considerable modification – before it is discussed with the little girl involved. Besides, my 'One-and-Only', day after tomorrow, Miss Cassey will be grown and you, in your dotage, will be left with a pony to ride."

"Oh. Well, maybe that should go on the 'Options' side of the paper."

"Very wise decision."

They had no illusions that all would go smoothly and without angst in the immediate future. Though they were enjoying day-dreaming and planning for the future, there were more pressing issues to be dealt with.

Matt was going to have to put in a lot of extra time at the office, gathering up loose ends from his recent absenteeism and gradually winning his way back into a place of respect among the employees. Many of them had heard only bits and pieces of his whereabouts the last few weeks. All they knew for sure was that he was missing and they were there working.

Anne fully understood the spot he was in and she understood, also, how he had gotten into that spot. She was grateful and had told him many times, but each time, he had assured her that he would have done it again if "the whole world was going to collapse around his feet."

Now, however, it was *her* turn to help *him*. She would act cheerful and excited about moving soon to the farm to get ready for school. She would write him long letters – every day – so he would have them to read at night before bed. She would *seldom* text him during the day because that would be an interruption. She would make this the *best year ever* at school and she would make their week-ends together some of their *best times ever*. (Those plans went on her mental list, but not on the paper.)

They planned to alternate week-ends at the farm or in town and would attend whosever church was near. It would be enjoyable and enlightening to experience such diverse approaches to God's way and God's family.

Gradually, Anne would sketch out her ideas for remodeling the farm house and Matt would assign one of the interns at the company the job of drawing the schematics during the next week.

They would not, however, start construction until Anne was through with school and at home to oversee. "I have learned, in my years of moving about in a man's world, there is only one creature more dangerous than a man with a chainsaw – and that is a man with a power-nailer," she stated. "They both need constant supervision. What the one can't cut down and haul off, the other one will nail down never to be moved again."

When they drove into the driveway at the farm, the back door opened and Matt saw his new brother-in-law for the first time. Within seconds, his preconceived image of "kid brother" vanished. Here was a full-grown, robust, weather-seasoned young man, larger, stronger and more well-developed than a professional architect could ever hope to be. Andrew wore jeans and work boots and a T-shirt stretched over bulging muscles – with a wide smile that would make Hollywood envious. He opened Anne's door and helped her out of the car. He swung her around in a bear hug. Matthew Stuart Breckenridge, was completely intimidated. But not for long.

Andrew came around the car and grabbed Matt's hand with both of his and said, "So, this is the man I am forever indebted to. I am proud to meet you. Welcome! Come inside and tell me all about this creature you have married and taken away from me."

Immediately, Matt remembered when Anne had told him, "Andrew is nothing like you and a lot like you. You will like him and he, you."

Becca had driven into town to pick up the twins who were coming in on a shuttle flight. She had baked a pound cake and made lemonade. As the afternoon wore on, they devoured all of it. After all the greetings and hugs, the conversation fluctuated between the six excited people. While everyone was eager to hear everything, they carefully steered away from the dreadful accident which had precipitated the whole thing.

Eventually, the conversation turned a bit "girlie" when Julia asked about the wedding and Becca divulged that she and Andrew were thinking about starting their family. Andrew glanced at Matt and noticed his eyes somewhat glazed over. He said, "Would you like to hop in the jeep and take a little run around the farm?"

Matt turned a 'thumbs -up'.

The two men remained quiet while they drove slowly from field to field. Matt would ask a question – Andrew would answer it. Andrew was impressed by how truly interested and eager to learn Matt was. At one point, Matt turned to him and said "I can sense that you really know and love this way of life, but please be patient with me. It is so foreign to me, I am completely awed."

Andrew acknowledged, "As I would be in your profession. I guess we'll always have lots to talk about, won't we?"

Matt grinned "Oh, yeah. No doubt about that. But know this – I have no intention of interfering here. Anne completely trusts you, so I do as well."

Once they had encompassed the entire farm and ended up in front of the shop, Andrew shut off the jeep and hopped out. Matt followed.

"Come into my office, said the spider to the fly", Andrew said. "It's the crumbiest little office that ever you did spy," he added, misquoting the little nursery rhyme.

Inside, there was room for storage of the smaller farm equipment like mowers and lawn tractors, as well as plenty of room for making large repairs – welding, anvils and motor hoists. A work-bench sat along one wall. A huge assortment of tools, large and small, hung from the other walls. But, in the front corner of the building, was a small room sectioned off and insulated which Andrew had made into his office.

They settled, fore and aft of an old wooden desk, into rickety wood office chairs that had been resurrected from who knows where.

Andrew explained, "There are a lot of *full-out, high-power, fun times* on a farm and many *quietly blessed, reflective times,* but when there is work to do, it's *Butts and Elbows!* This little room is where Anne or I sometimes come to be quiet and pray for help – and sometimes come to organize the B's -*n*- E's time."

Matt lifted his head in acknowledgement. "B's -*n*- E's, eh?". A light bulb went off in his head, igniting a creative spark and....

Two weeks later, when Matt arrived at the farm mid-morning, Andrew came out of the shop to greet him. Matt reached into the back seat of the car and pulled out a rough-sawed piece of cedar about three feet long. He handed it to his brother-in-law with a grin.

"Something to hang above your office door," he said.

Andrew raised his eyebrows, looked at the board and then burst out laughing. "Perfect!" he said. "Let me grab a hammer and some nails."

He nailed the piece of cedar above the door, then stepped back to look at it. He punched the air with his fist and shouted, "Yes!"

The sign said, THE BEE'S KNEES.

That evening the family had a wiener roast out in the edge of the back yard. As they were sitting around the fire, watching the sunset, Julie quietly asked Anne, "Is Bubby coming for a hot dog?"

Anne shook her head. "I doubt it."

Julie wrapped a well-doctored hot dog in a napkin, grabbed a cold soda, hopped on the four-wheeler and took off toward the woods.

Matt noticed, but no one gave any explanation, so he didn't ask. After dusk, while they listened to the evening sounds and watched several V's of wild geese glide across an almost full moon, Julie slipped back among them without a word. Again, no explanation – no questions.

Who – or what – and where – is this Bubby? Matt wondered.

Chapter Fourteen

Sunday afternoon, not more than five miles out of Spring Valley, headed for Maplegrove, Matt could stand it no longer. "So . . . who's Bubby?"

Anne grinned from ear to ear. "Are you in for a very long story?"

"If it's about Bubby, yes."

She turned toward him, drew her knees up into the seat and leaned against the car door. "Do you believe in fairy tales? Real, live fairy tales?"

He winked. "Try me."

"His name is Reginald Bernard Leopold Petrovsky. He appeared out of nowhere one day during strawberry season. He came – he stayed – and he forgot to leave."

Matt concentrated on the road and settled in for a good story.

"One day, in June, the kids and I were picking strawberries when we looked up to see this bearded, disheveled man and his little dog standing off in the distance, watching us. The pup was sitting quietly beside him, his tongue lolling out, just looking at us – but his little tail was wagged furiously. He watched the twins who were probably about seven at the time. He looked like it was all he could do to keep from running to one of them.

"I didn't have enough sense to be uneasy, but Andrew was wary and picked up the hoe at the end of the row.

"The man spoke to us softly, 'Do you need help with the pickin'?' he asked. 'I've picked berries plenty.'

"Are you looking for work?" I asked.

"'Mostly just a drink of water, if I might,' he said.

"I told the twins to get the man a glass of water and a little pan of water for the dog. I wanted to get them away from the situation, anyway. We just continued to stare at each other, neither of us knowing what to do next.

"When the twins came back, the pup was so thirsty, he almost knocked the pan of water out of Nathan's hand. The man took the glass from Julia and downed it in one long gulp. Then, he bowed gallantly to her and said, "Thank you very much, princess.'

"The dog licked Nathan's hands and wiggled up next to his feet."

I smiled at the man and asked him, 'Do you know how to pick strawberries without moaning and groaning and complaining like my current helpers do?"

"He grinned, 'Oh, yes ma'am. I'm very quiet when I pick.'

"I handed him a picking basket and bent over to pick again. Andrew took my cue and started on his row again. The twins forgot all about berries and plopped down to play with the dog. We finished the patch without their help.

"As Andrew pulled the strawberry wagon toward the house, I stretched my back and asked him, 'Would you like a sandwich and some iced tea, sir?' Matt, the man acted and spoke with such polite dignity, I never doubted he was a gentleman. Not once in those couple of hours. As we stood there, I looked into his eyes and I saw gratitude and hope and kindness and . . .oh, I don't know. All the things you *expect* to see in a good man's eyes."

"Did you ever consider how *dangerously naïve* that was of you?" Matt asked.

"Absolutely. That's why Andrew and I have never told the whole story to anyone before. Well, by now, he has probably told Becca, his wife. But I have not – only you, now. Everyone else thinks he is just a man we hired to help around the place."

"Anyway?" Matt prodded.

"Anyway, we ate chicken salad sandwiches and drank quarts and quarts of iced tea at the picnic table in the shade. That's when he told me his atrocious name. "And when he told the children his pup's name was Spot, he kind of rolled his eyes at me and whispered, 'Not very original, is it?' He looked away and then added, 'I remembered that name from a First Reader I had when I was a small child.' He squatted on his heels and stroked the dog's ears and chuckled, 'It would seem that my little friend here is *lacking* a proper name, while I am somewhat *over-burdened* in that regard.'

"He didn't discuss his history, where he had come from or where he was headed. At one point, I asked him where he slept at night and he said he had a tent. He said, 'It's in my pack at the end of the driveway. I didn't bring it into the yard because I didn't want to frighten you,' he added.

"The outcome of our visit was that he could pitch his tent out by the barn and we would furnish him and his little rat terrier food, if he would stay during berry season and pick for me. He was pleased. I was appreciative.

"He never told me what to call him, but I heard him say once to Nathan, 'Bubby, if you throw the pup a bit of bread, he will dance for you.'

"I noticed that the kids started referring to *him* as Bubby – so that's who he came to be to us. He seemed to like the name for himself, but he still calls all children Bubby, too.

"Picking had to be done every other day. He seemed to know that already, and on those mornings, he had everything ready – even the kids -- by the time the dew was off and time to begin. After lunch, we hauled the fresh berries to the Farmer's Market in town, but Bubby never went with us. He seemed to be completely self-sufficient.

"One day, he did ask me for a bar of soap. I think he took his baths after dark at the pump where we filled the stock tank. And a couple times I noticed some clothes stretched out on the grass in the sunshine to dry. I honestly think he ate nothing but what we supplied him.

"One time, I asked him if I could bring him something from the store. He looked embarrassed and I was sorry I had asked. 'I'm entirely fine', he answered quietly and could not – or *would* not – look me in the eye. I decided then and there, whatever I was able to do for him must be done *with* him and not *for* him and must preserve his dignity at all costs."

"Dignity is a powerful thing", Matt replied. "It's what sustains a man when pride has deserted him completely."

Anne continued, "As the strawberry crop began to dwindle, early one morning, I noticed Bubby hoeing in the garden. Later he brought in peas and green beans he had picked.

"I think the Lord helped me to understand that the man was, in his way, asking me if he could still be useful to us and if he could stay. I knew he loved the farm. I had seen him sitting at the lake watching the ducks or walking in the woods with Spot bouncing along beside him. And, once, when I couldn't sleep, I was sitting on the back step and, in the bright moonlight, I saw him lying on his back in the pasture, just looking up at the sky. He was *experiencing* the same night sky that has always been my balm in hard times.

"Matt, I *had* to think of a way to ask him to stay. . . . and the Lord helped me again".

Ever since we had owned the farm – ever since I was a child, really – there had been an old building behind the house. It is probably about 8 X 12 feet and was originally a smoke house where meat was smoked and stored. Then, after refrigeration and before automatic washers, it had been a wash house. In fact, it still had the old wringer washer in it. But it was an eyesore and used for nothing but a dumping place for unwanted stuff too good to throw away. I had wanted that thing torn down or moved behind the barn forever!

"I asked our farmer if he thought he and his tractor/loader could move it to the woods. He agreed to try. He shored it up with timbers and tied it together with cables and lifted the whole thing off its foundation with his tractor. The Lord prompted me to ask Bubby to superintend the process and decide somewhere to put it. They moved it into the edge of the woods where you saw it the other day.

"Oh, what a sight! I thought every moment the whole thing would collapse.

"Later, he asked me, 'What are you planning for the smoke house?'

"I said, 'I don't know. I'm just glad to have it out of the yard. Now I can make that rock garden I've been wanting. I guess we could store stuff in it out there. It's too good a building to just let it deteriorate. In the meantime, with fall coming on, if you want to put your things in there, Spot would keep the mice out of it at least.'

"Bubby thought that was a workable plan -- and he's been there ever since.

"Little by little, through the years, we have needed to store things in there. Like the old iron bed I couldn't bear to throw away and the antique table and chairs when we remodeled the kitchen. But never once have we *offered* them to Bubby – we just store them in his building. And never once has he asked to use any of it – he just uses it because it's there. We understand each other and we respect each other.

"He has been a part of us for eleven years. And we need him."

They were both quiet for some time. Finally, Matt reflected, "I believe every word of your fairy tale, but I have to admit – I am intensely curious. Do you know absolutely *nothing* else about him?"

Anne bristled slightly. "Oh, yes. I know more," she smiled at him. "I'm not a *total innocent,* you know.

"The next morning, I took Bubby's iced-tea glass to the sheriff, John Colter – he's a good friend of mine."

Matt rolled his eyes. "Why am I not surprised?"

She laughed, "Anyway – he ran fingerprints on him, as well as his name through every legal source he had available."

"And? Hurry up here, will you?"

"And -- Bubby has no criminal record, not even a parking ticket. But – a very extensive and enlightening military record."

Chapter Fifteen

With Labor Day the coming Tuesday, Anne had two days off from school and decided to drive back to Maplegrove with Matt. Though that meant an extra trip for him, it gave the two a rare opportunity to visit. She was sorry she had not expected this conversation so had not brought along the dossier on Bubby the sheriff had given her. However, she told him the basics and he could read the details later.

R. B. L. Petrovsky had come to the United States from Romania in 1940. He came alone. Beyond that, most personal and family history had been expunged from his military record – which frustrated and aggravated the good sheriff until he read further into the man's military service record. Then he understood fully. All ties to family and other personal connections were erased by Intel for their own protection.

R. Petrov had been trained and served as a Green Beret. He later was re-assigned to Army Intelligence where his fluency in multiple languages proved invaluable. He worked under several different code names – all classified. He served in multiple locations during two wars and supposed peacetime and was honorably discharged after seventeen years of service to his adopted country. He was awarded several Army Achievement and Commendation Awards.

Anne added, "John spent a couple hours with Bubby out on the lake fishing one day. He did not even *try* to be incognito. He wore his uniform and badge and introduced himself to Bubby as Sheriff Colter. Given the stranger's background, he knew better than to pretend. But they had a good visit – no talking, just fishing. Caught a couple good-sized sunfish and fried them on the spot.

"The sheriff reassured Andrew and me -- and has left him alone since then. Matt, Bubby is not a vagrant, he is not loitering -- he is a resident farm-hand."

Matt thought about it all and finally he said, "You know what I think? I think his military experience is *why* and *when* he gave up his identity. And I think he is uncomfortable – and perhaps even fearful – about letting anyone know who he is."

"And I think something else," Anne added. "I think he may have had a royalty background before he came to America. The man has been formally schooled and regally trained! You will discover that for yourself in time. I'm so glad you will have an opportunity to befriend him."

"I truly do look forward to it," he said.

Matthew had not forgotten one of his primary goals on their original must do list. He wanted with all his heart, to see a closeness and sincere friendship between his mother and Anne. It was no secret that Claire was the reluctant one. Anne was longing to win Claire's approval, but she realized that friendship cannot be forced. If it is not natural, it is not friendship at all. One day, after Claire had come home from her self-imposed exile, Anne made a suggestion to her worried husband.

"Let's have a family weekend here at the farm. Let's invite your parents, Papa B, Mark and his family. I'll ask the twins to come too, and, of course, Andrew and Becca.

"I'll organize it well and we'll have a grand time just relaxing and getting acquainted. I know how to do it. I've done it lots of times with gangs from the church and the kids' youth group.

"We'll ask your folks to bring their motorhome to stay in – as though we *need* them to for the sake of space. That way, your mother will have her own space if she needs to pull back. Papa B can have the downstairs bedroom and adjoining bath. The rest of us can *bunk, bag and pallet*. What do you think?"

"What do I think?" he repeated. "I'll get on it first thing Monday morning! I'll talk to Dad and Mark and . . ."

"No, sweetheart. Please let me. It will be important for the invitation to come from me. That, my darling, is the way women's social minds work. Just trust me on this, okay?"

"I concede. I have no intention of trying to understand a woman's mind – social or otherwise."

The invitations were issued by phone – woman to woman -- and all responses were positive. Claire was sweet and polite and gracious, but she agreed that she and Breck would be happy to bring their own accommodations.

Breck and Matt were hopeful, Papa was agreeable, Mark's family was excited – especially about the prospect of sleeping bags. The twins thought they were really too busy, but understood how important this was to Anne, and Becca was eager to help in all preparations.

The whole week-end was *casually organized* by Anne, as was her natural motif. The only posted schedules were sign-up sheets on the two upstairs bathroom doors for shower times (15 minutes) and tub times (30 minutes). The first-floor half-bath was *catch as catch can and luck to you*.

For breakfasts, the kitchen was well-stocked with cereal, toast supplies, juices, milk and coffee – even some cinnamon rolls while they lasted. It was come-and-go-as-you-please. There *was* bacon and eggs in the fridge, but no one *dared* raise *that* kind of smell for fear of attracting a crowd.

At noon, the women pulled an endless supply of sandwich-makings, fresh fruit and cookies from secret hiding places – and, from somewhere, a crock-pot of potato or chicken-noodle soup mysteriously appeared.

Supper was a different thing all together. Friday evening, the ladies prepared fried chicken, potatoes and gravy, biscuits, green vegetables, corn-on-the-cob, strawberry shortcake and pitchers of iced tea. The dining room table was extended, which allowed the kids to sit at the *big* table.

Saturday supper? That was a saga! The men were responsible for the menu and all preparations. No ordering-out was allowed. They did, however, find a way to cheat. They bribed Ardyth to supervise. They told her they would catch a bunch of fish for the meat. They decided on potato salad, deviled eggs, watermelon, no green vegetables, and homemade ice-cream for dessert. If they caught the fish, would she bring the rest of the stuff?

But Ardyth was not naïve. She took the challenge and brought the *groceries* but did NOT prepared the dishes. She brought along a small turkey to stick in the oven, "Just in case." She told them, "I'll teach one of you how to put the hurt on a bird and you can teach me how to find my way around a fish. I've always wanted to know how to fillet a fish with a jack-knife." She supervised, instructed and bossed, but our bad boys had to do their own cooking. Even Papa B made his heretofore unknown famous recipe for lemonade – with sliced lemons and a potato masher.

They fried their fish on the grill outside and set up picnic tables. They spread red-checked paper table covers and she *did allow* paper plates and plastic glasses.

Claire circulated among the amateur chefs for a bit and then declared, "I can stand this chaos no longer. I'm going inside the RV and pretend I don't know any of you!" She glanced uncertainly at Anne and asked, "Would you care to join me?"

That surprised Anne a bit --she was actually enjoying watching -- but she felt compelled to accept the invitation. "That will be a profound relief to *this* madness," she said. The two women disappeared, but anyone observing would have seen them watching the activity from the RV window.

As they were standing together, looking out the window, Claire said, "I'd love to be a mouse in that kitchen right now. What about you?"

Anne hooked her pinkie finger toward Claire. "Secret?" she asked. "I have my phone on the cabinet behind the cookie jar, recording the whole thing."

Claire hooked her pinkie around Anne's. "Sworn secret," she said.

When, eventually, the food was spread on the table, the men gloated and took pictures. The women bragged on them. It was fantastic -- and great fun.

Sunday noon – before everyone headed for home – it was a giant smorgasbord of left-overs -- or, as Cassey called them, *re-runs*.

The whole week-end was a huge success. Even the one tense moment ended with a new understanding and a new gentle relationship.

At the table Friday night, Julia issued a challenge to Papa B that he could not walk away from. She sat next to him and he had asked her what she planned to do the coming summer between classes. She told him she was planning to head to New York for lab studies on the homeless in the large city.

Then, with the passion of youth, she laid down the gauntlet. "If all the wealth in the world was more evenly distributed instead of hoarded, there would be no homelessness.

"Even the Bible says, money is the root of all evil," she admonished.

Papa bristled, "Listen well, my fledgling crusader. You've got your scripture all wrong. The verse says "the *love* of money is the root of all evil.

"It was God Himself who blessed Abraham of old with great wealth and it was God Himself who blessed Joseph with power and position and wealth. And why? So that they could accomplish God's own purposes.

"When God Almighty knows a man's heart is right, He knows, also, that He can give him great wealth to use for the Kingdom – and it will be done. If there was no need for material wealth in this world to accomplish God's purposes, then, my dear, there would *be* no material wealth. You can count on it. The Lord does not bless needlessly."

He paused, but before she could collect her next comments, he said, "You're not the first idealistic innocent who has attacked me with their disdain of money. But then guess, little one, who is the first evil money monger they come to for financial support for one of their magnanimous projects to save the world.

"Who do think built the Veterans' Memorial Building on that university you're attending? Did you think it was a veteran who paid for it? If it *was* a vet, it was one who God had blessed with wealth. Because, it was *money* that built that building to honor their sacrifice."

"Okay, Okay." Julia conceded, "But we need to do more than just build a building in their honor – a building probably not one of them have ever been in. We need to get them off the streets and into homes with beds and warm blankets and full refrigerators."

She paused, "You've probably got blankets in your closets that haven't been unfolded since your wife died. I wouldn't be surprised if . . ."

As the silence of Julia's unfinished sentence became more intense, Anne made a move to interrupt her sister and issue a reprimand to cool the situation, but Andrew laid his hand on her arm and nodded in the direction of Nathan.

Nathan cleared his throat and spoke. "Jules?". With that one word, he gave his twin sister a warning shot across the bow that said, "That's far enough."

Julia stopped, midsentence. Her fiery eyes glared at him then gradually softened. She glanced down at her plate. After a long, silent moment, she looked up at Papa B and said, "I'm sorry, Mr. Breckenridge. That was over the top and out of line. Oh, I don't know what else. I'm sorry." She lowered her head again and brushed non-existent crumbs from her lap.

Papa grinned and said, "It's okay, lassie. I've been sassed by sweet ladies before."

He stood up and pointed a finger at her. "Tell you what. I'll make you a deal.

"You find yourself a homeless veteran who is willing to work four hours a day for his keep and I'll give him a groundskeeper job at my home, a place to stay, a full refrigerator and a bed – and a couple folded blankets, too. Deal?"

Julia stuck out her hand. "Deal," she said. "And sir. . . may I call you 'Papa'?"

His only response was a gruff, embarrassed, "Humph".

Julia jumped up and hugged him like an excited little kid.

Chapter Sixteen

A gradual unifying of the greater family unit occurred slowly and with sincere effort. Not surprising, considering these two groups of human beings could not have been more different, their sole common bond was their belief and trust in the Lord God Almighty.

The Whitfields welcomed the friendship of Matthew's family, but remained tentative about what might be expected of them in the future. The Breckenridges welcomed the warm embrace of friendship from Anne's family and enjoyed their fresh, open-hearted acceptance. Even Claire, who had, at first, built such harsh barriers against the relationship, was too fine a woman with too much character to hold grudges toward the beautiful, intelligent, talented young woman who had captured her son's heart.

Breck accepted the fact that Claire had dropped out of sight after the spontaneous wedding. He smiled benignly when his father grilled him about it. "That's the way Claire handles conflict, Dad. She suffers alone. She prefers to withdraw and let the disagreement die a natural death, rather than talk it to death. She'll show up one of these days, contrite, mended and stronger for it."

Unexpectedly, the traumatic impact of a serious conflict in the young marriage presented itself with heat and intensity.

In his last communique before Anne travelled to Maplegrove one week-end, Matt said, "I can't wait to tell you something I've been doing. You're going to be so surprised, but you'll *love* it!"

Well, surprised she was, but *Love it* was not the notable reaction.

"Are you ready for this?" he asked.

Anne laughed. "For goodness sake, get on with it before I choke on my curiosity!"

Matt shoved his plate of uneaten food back and leaned both elbows on the table.

"Do you remember Brandon Forsythe you met at the company Christmas party?"

Anne nodded.

"Well, one night last week" Matt continued, "I was working late. My phone rang and it was Brandon's wife, Ashley. She asked me how soon it would be before Brandon would be leaving for home. She was fixing a six-month anniversary dinner for him and wanted to know when to expect him. It hit me like a ton of bricks! He had told her he was going to work late – but he wasn't!

"I guess I hesitated a bit too long, and she asked if she could speak to him. "I had to tell her, 'He's not here, Ashley.' Then she asked me when he left."

Matt looked stricken. "Annie, what could I tell her?" He looked down at the table and fiddled with his silverware. "I tried to act nonchalant and told her, "I think I know where he is. I'll get him and scoot him right home to you. And . . . happy anniversary, Ashley."

Matt stopped. He looked at his wife with pain in his eyes. "I found him. I knew where he would be. Where he had often been in the evenings before they were married. Where he had sworn he would not go again *after* they were married. He was at the 'Hit and Run'".

"It's a beer joint?" Anne asked.

"It's a beer garden out front, a bar and game room inside and a supposed *private party room* in the back. Anyway, I talked him into leaving and took him home."

"And?"

"And -- I don't know. He was sorry, of course. They're working on it. I think they'll eventually be able to heal the scars. But that's not the exciting thing I want to tell you!

"I've been thinking a lot about those men and women who frequent places like that. They're victims, really. Some of them are victims of the disease of alcoholism, of course --some of other things. Lack of training or wrong example when they were kids, no self-worth, not enough self-control, no purpose in their life -- and most of all, no Lord walking with them in their lives.

"So, here it is! I've decided to give a couple nights a week to them. I'm going to go to the 'Hit and Run' and visit with one or more of them each of those nights."

"You're *what*?"

"I think I can make a difference in some young lives by showing them that *somebody* cares and by offering other ways to handle their difficulties beside alcohol."

"You're going to actually spend time at the Hit and Run?"

"Yes! So, what do you think?"

Anne continued to look at him, but said nothing. What she *didn't* say hung between them. He heard it – and, truthfully, her reaction surprised him.

Everything was quiet – too quiet.

This was the first time Anne had not been his advocate, encouraging him to be what and all he could be. He felt hurt and disappointed. He slowly pushed his chair back from the table and rose. Barely above a whisper, he said, "I'm sorry, Annie", and walked quietly from the room.

That began a situation neither of them knew how to deal with. They both knew their dinner was over. Sleep would be non-existent until peace and understanding reigned in their blessed home once more.

Anne half-heartedly cleared the table and covered the uneaten food. Then she stepped into the other room where Matt sat with his elbows on his knees, his head down. She sat on the floor in front of him.

"Why would you want to subject yourself to that kind of environment? Is there no other place you can make contact with any of those people?"

Matt stared at her wide eyes. "That's where *those people*, as you call them, are!"

"I'm sorry. I didn't mean it like it sounded. You're right, of course. Do you know others like them? Is there no other way you can have an influence with some of them besides going to the Hit and Run?"

"Yes, I know of others – some are our employees. I know *why* one or two of them feel compelled to hang out there. That's why I think I might help them. That's why I *know* I *can* help them. That's why I am *going* to help them."

Breck, Matthew's father, could have warned Anne, had he been available, that her husband would occasionally reach a point where he would not be budged, as had happened when he tried to deter him from marrying *her*. But Breck was not here – and our Matthew had reached that point. Fortunately, Anne recognized it.

She laid her hand on his and prayed silently.

After a while, Matt said. "I have told you my *'Whys'*. Now, you tell me yours."

"The Bible tells us to abstain from the appearance of evil and this plan seems to fall into that category. And it also admonishes 'Do not imitate what is evil'."

But Matt replied, "The Bible also tells us that we 'are the light of the world'. How can we be light to a dark world if we never go where the darkness is?"

"Sometimes, those of us who have been Christians since we were young, go through our whole lives without seeing, first hand, the joy of a lost soul discovering Christ for the first time. I want to do that. And I can't do that if I stay cloistered inside a 'brotherhood of believers'.

I want to be a part of the experience when a hurting person meets Jesus face-to-face and really sees Him for who He is."

Ann smiled, "You're cheating. You're rebutting my arguments without hearing me out."

"Sorry", he said.

She continued, "Is there no chance that the influence might go the wrong way? How long can you be there before you might be tempted to identify more closely with them – to prove that you are one of them – that you fully understand their troubles – to make them feel more at ease around you?"

Matt stood, took a few steps and turned toward her. "I have enough self-control not to take a drink of alcohol – which, by the way, does not appeal to me in the least. Do you doubt my faith that the Lord will help me?"

"I don't doubt, for a minute, your intentions, Matt. You will remember – I was completely at your mercy for a recent period of time, my precious darling. But Proverbs also warns, 'Do not be wise in your own eyes; fear the Lord and shun evil.' And that, from the wisest man in world."

"Matt countered, "Since we're both claiming alliance with scripture, I will remind you that Jesus, Himself, said, 'It is not the healthy who need a doctor, but the sick.'"

"I believe that, of course. It's the *location* of the *treatment* that I worry about."

"And the reliability of the doctor?" he asked testily.

"Oh, Matt, I . . ."

In the end, there was only tentative acceptance of each other's conviction. They could not resolve what were intractable differences. He was more determined than ever -- she was unyielding. They merely *agreed* to *disagree*.

The concluding skirmish, though, changed nothing – and everything. Anne's parting shot was full of meaning, "When you go, take an angel with you."

Chapter Seventeen

The following year was a year of completions and beginnings.

Anne finished her school term while the construction crew finished the remodel of the farm house. Papa B officially retired from the company board of directors and Breck became President and CEO.

The old gentleman came to the office only when something slipped out in family conversations that he didn't like. Then he would show up un-announced and poke around. It was unspoken – but it was expected -- that his questions, comments and opinions, no matter how abrasive, would be respected and treated with courtesy – if *not* compliance. At the farm, Bubby seemed vaguely interested in Matt's presence and had made tenuous overtures in that direction. Matt was determined to pay Bubby a visit on *his* turf to reassure him that he wanted him to remain a part of the farm.

The mutual respect between Claire and Anne grew gradually and naturally. Neither forced it – but both wanted it. They became antiquing cohorts, often spending Saturdays shopping for bargains . . . or *not-necessarily* bargains. Anne furnished and decorated the fifth-floor apartment of The Breck, now the home of Mr. and Mrs. Matthew Stuart Breckenridge, IV.

Matt and Anne began counting the weeks until the birth of their firstborn in late December. The two of them decided they did not want to know the gender of the baby ahead of time. At their first appointment with Ted Milton, the doctor said, "Well, boy or girl, you should name the baby 'Cement' because that's what this baby is going to be for the Breckenridge and Whitfield families."

On occasion, Anne found a need to stop into Matt's office. She always made a point to stop by the employees' lounge to visit with whomever happened to be there. One such time, a secretary from the main office was noticeably stressed. Anne sat down across the table with her coffee. She asked, "Juanita, isn't it?" The secretary nodded. "Have you worked here long?" Anne asked.

The young lady responded, "Not long enough, I'm afraid. I think I may have to quit and I don't want to at all. I *need* this job."

"I'm sorry," Anne said. "How did that come about?"

"I've lost my babysitter and" . . . with a sad smile, "I can't find another one close by that I'm comfortable with for my two little ones. Does that sound too persnickety?"

"Oh, not at all. I often think that's the hardest part of a young mother's having to work at an outside job. I understand completely."

She paused and then asked, "How about if you and I pray about this?"

"Here and now?" the woman asked.

Anne held out her hand to her. "Here and now," she said.

As they held hands, Anne prayed, "Dear Lord, this mother needs your help. She loves her children and she wants what's best for them. Lord, she's in a bind here and needs your loving help because you know more about love than anyone else. And, Father, let me know if there is any way I can help, too. In our Savior's name, Amen"

As she rose from the table, she hugged Juanita and gave her a card with her phone number on it. "Call me when you hear back from the Lord – and I'll do the same. OK?"

That evening she mentioned the conversation to Matt, He remarked, "Yes, I was afraid she might leave us – and I'm sorry. She's *senior* in that office and knows what she's doing. She's a good motivator and leader. The others look up to her."

Anne said, "What if I kept her babies for her. We're close by the office, I'm good with little ones and I'm sort of at loose ends since I've retired. I'm *retired*, but I'm not *tired!* What do you think?"

"Whoa, Trigger!" Have you thought that through? You're talking about a *major* commitment here, kiddo. What if you and Mom wanted to hit some antique sales? What if you needed to drive out to the farm for something? What if I wanted you to hit the road with me to a job site?"

Anne considered these possibilities. "You're right," she said. "It *would* be a drastic change in my – our – lifestyle. But then, of course, that *is* going to happen very soon anyway, of our own choosing."

Matt suggested, "Let's give ourselves two days to think about it. If something else doesn't turn up for her in the meantime, then we'll decide. okay?"

"Okay," Anne agreed. "But a question comes to mind that begs an answer. Who is it who is usually the cautious one here and who the spontaneous one?"

A smiling, "Ah, yes." was his only response.

Two days of discussion and two nights of restless sleep later, the two of them called on Juanita and got acquainted with the children. After visiting with them, Anne made her offer. She laid out her credentials and plans, along with the future after their own baby was born. The young mother was ecstatic and accepted the proposal on the spot.

Thus, another of the year's fresh starts – one that would prove to be the beginning of something much bigger than any of them had anticipated.

The Breckenridge Corporation was a small community within itself and, as in most small towns, the grapevine was robust and productive. Before long, Anne had received childcare inquiries from other staff members as well.

With trepidation, she finagled an encounter with her father-in-law, Corporate CEO and his friend, Dr. Ted Milton, during lunch at their club. She hit them with a proposition. When they took her up on it, it scared her to death.

She went through all the phases of attempting a challenge bigger than she anticipated. First, excitement, then hesitation and doubt, ending with enthusiasm mixed with fear. She confided to Matt, "Once in a while, the Lord spills us out of our easy chair and says, 'Here! Grab hold of this!'"

The outcome was a company-sponsored day-care for employees' children and use of the empty first-floor apartment in The Breck. None of them could have imagined how this *hatchling* of an idea would one day *soar like an eagle*.

The day-care grew to encompass more and more of the first floor of the building. Claire and Anne borrowed the company van and haunted every available source of used baby beds, pint-sized tables and chairs, even potty seats. Julia spread buckets of nature colored paint on any exposed wall. Nathan designed a computer program so they could remain *fiscally responsible*. Mark, in true CFO style, issued a memo – employees would have the option of paying the current per diem rate or receiving a 'per-child' reduction to their salary. Dr. Ted volunteered to oversee compliance with health and safety standards. Matt and Breck watched, listened, encouraged, smiled, hauled, lifted and lugged whatever needed to be done.

Even Papa B got involved. Anne invited him and George (his new groundskeeper) to come see and give us some ideas. She just happened to have apple pie on hand and served them some – with Vanilla Bean ice cream and ridiculously strong, black coffee – the way they liked it.

Her request to give us some ideas may have been a mistake. Papa pronounced the whole thing an outrageous operation. "In my day, when this company began, people took care of their own kids. They left them with grandparents or aunts or neighbors – or, better still, the women stayed home and took care of them themselves."

But she later found him sitting on the sofa, kids piled all over him, telling them The Three Bears, with all the appropriate bear voices.

Chapter Eighteen

Three against one makes for a somewhat lop-sided vote – but an excellent balance of power when the need arises.

Anne, with the support of Matt and Breck, asked Claire to assume management of The Bee Hive and serve as Chairperson of the Board of Directors.

"Ouch! Speak of being dumped out of your easy chair! Is there no one else?" Claire asked.

"I haven't looked or asked," Anne said emphatically. "We don't want anyone else. No one else is as uniquely qualified as you are." She laughed. "And, by the way, the word was *spilled,* not *dumped*."

"What on earth could you possibly mean – uniquely qualified?"

"You're a Christian, first and foremost. You're a mother – and only a mother, a Christian mother, can see deeply enough to understand the full impact of what these babies need. You have the authority and flexibility to shuffle your priorities and make room for this ministry.

"You were created – by the great God Almighty Himself – with the intelligence and compassion to do justice to the scope of this challenge. Many people would have one or the other, but few have both.

"And . . .you have the eyes for it!"

Claire's eyebrows shot upward, while she stared at Anne in total confusion.

"Eyes?"

Anne chuckled. "Yes, eyes. Such, deep, expressive eyes that could melt the coldest vendor's heart -- or demand, without words, obedience from a belligerent twelve-year-old scamp, or say to a frightened child, 'I love you so much'. I'm afraid, my dear Mrs. Breckenridge, that those eyes give away secrets of your very soul."

She laughed, "I have been both victim and recipient of what your soul has to say – and I do so admire you for that blessing to me."

Claire smiled slightly, shaking her head in disbelief at the intuition of this remarkable young woman, and stared out the window in thought.

Anne pushed her luck and continued. "I know you are busy – but there's a reason why leaders are always busy. We're asking you if you will make the sacrifice to give direction and leadership to this opportunity to serve Him.

"I feel a little like old Mordecai in the Bible, when he said to Queen Esther, 'Who knows but that you were born for such a time as this.'"

Claire glanced back at Anne and grinned. "As I recall, *that* proposal was a matter of life and death."

They laughed, then Claire looked directly – *very* directly at Anne.

She said, "I will do this – on one condition . . . that you begin to call me Mom – or Claire – whichever you're most comfortable with. I feel like we are truly friends, so Claire would be fine. But Matt calls me Mom . . .and *dare NOT call me Claire!*" she warned, as she looked sideways at him.

"I would be honored to call you Mom," Anne said.

Claire had opportunity to use intelligence *and* authority *and* eyes before long. The city sent notice that, in reference to the application for an operating license, Inspector Clemons would be arriving on Tuesday at 10:00 a.m.

He came. He saw. And he began to find fault.

"There are supposed to be bumper posts in front of the parking space by the building to prevent someone from crashing into the building."

Claire smiled understandingly. "I can completely understand that," she said. "However, I have never yet seen a seven-year old boy who could resist climbing onto a three-foot bumper post and immediately falling off. In the interest of safety, we must not create hazardous situations where they might get hurt. I trust you understand."

The inspector checked an OK on his worksheet.

Again, he complained, "That microwave should not be installed above the stove. It will need to be moved and an exhaust fan placed there, in case of a cooking fire."

Claire said, "You would have no way of knowing, Mr. Clemons, that the microwave has a full-power fan as part of the installation. And, in addition, the fan in the ceiling above the stove is also vented to the outside. That is unusual, I know, but we knew you would want it that way. Besides, for safety's sake, we have to keep the microwave higher than the children can reach."

After what seemed to Claire like a very long time they stood in the kitchen while Mr. Clemons mumbled to his paperwork. Claire prayed for patience. He pulled out his pocket-knife and cut a plastic band holding the sheaf of papers, when a little six-year-old boy sidled up to him and held up a big, red apple.

"Mithter," he said. "Pleath, thir. Could you cut up my apple? You thee, I can't bite it." He smiled. His two front teeth were missing.

The gentled and subdued man took the apple, cored it and cut it into slices with his pocket knife. Claire looked directly at him with raised eyebrows, innocently questioning eyes, and a knowing smile. The look that passed between them silently acknowledged that *that* little maneuver would be in direct conflict of *any* health standards of *any* city ordinance anywhere. He blinked, turned on his heal and walked out the door.

As he passed by her, he said, "I'll see you tomorrow at City Hall. 10:30 sharp. And bring your check book – there's a license fee."

Unintentionally, Matthew Stuart Breckenridge, Junior had initiated another step in the services of his so-called outrageous operation – adding *senior care*.

Someone made an innocent remark at the company summer picnic, "I wish there was a place where my mother could enjoy herself while I'm at work. She won't admit it, but I think she's lonely."

Anne remembered the picture of Papa B with the children and *the cerebral gears began to mesh*.

Why not? she thought.

"Why not?" she asked at the next Bee Hive Board meeting.

Among them, they could name several Breckenridge staff members who had an elderly parent living with them. In the lunch room, they had heard bits and pieces of the typical worries about leaving these vulnerable loved ones alone during the day.

Anne suggested, "Why not invite two or three of these seniors to stay at the Bee Hive during the day? They could interact with each other and with the children. They would have a good lunch and as much activity or rest as they wanted."

Matt asked, "Could we find two or three employees who would be willing to give it a try for six months? I think we should move slowly. This is a major step."

All agreed that they should start small with the goal to let it grow naturally by word of mouth throughout the company. Start small, think big.

Mark was cautious – which is the primary skill-set of a good accountant. His one comment, "When I think of the financial, legal, medical, regulatory challenges, my mind solidifies!"

Breck remained stoic. He stroked his chin, taking his time to think it through, then leaned forward with his arms on the table. Everyone waited. He looked directly at his two sons. "Matthew, you must spend a very minimal amount of time or thought on this project. It is your job to carry The Breckenridge Corporation successfully into the future. And Mark, I have every confidence in you. If this plan works, you can set it on solid ground as you have with every other idiotic thing the B's have undertaken."

Claire agreed to add seniors to the Hive on one condition – that Anne would supervise that side of the venture.

Anne, recognizing the cost of creativity, agreed. She knew daytime care for the elderly was a current social issue. She knew this was a good idea. She knew they could make it work.

Within two months, they had taken over the whole first floor of the building.

Chapter Nineteen

Can a broken heart give solace to a wounded soul? The second time Matt found Brandon out alone, he brought him home with him. He flushed him out with strong coffee and time and let him talk.

When the young man said in anger, "I can't help wondering if, against everything we have always believed, we had lived together a while before we got married, I would have found out that Ashley has some *major* intimacy hang-ups."

He ranted on. "I had always naively held the stupid ideal that couples should remain pure until after marriage. Ha! Not so! The wedding night just may be when you get more surprises than you bargained for."

"Oh, my friend," Matt said. "Never give up on what you know to be right when you're hurting or afraid."

But that's when Matt knew he was in over his head here. He did not encourage more talk. He did not want to know more of the issues which were tearing this young couple apart. Once the opportunity presented itself, Matt suggested he introduce the couple to the marriage counselor in Uncle Ted's family practice. And that's when Ashley told her story.

It was her step-brother. The one she had known since seventh grade when her mother remarried and his family moved in with them.

It was the step-brother two years older than her who had always been her big-brother-protector, had become her best friend, the one whom she fully trusted and whom she thought loved her.

It was the same brother who had chosen his college friends poorly and had changed. The same brother who caught her in the shower one evening when no one else was at home, had pulled her out of the shower and into his own room where his friends waited.

It was this brother who finally tired of watching and threw a blanket over her and said to the others, "Come on guys. Leave her alone." And then they left.

Matthew did not need to know the story. It was enough that Brandon and Ashley continued to work with the counselor for several weeks. But he *had* noticed a softening and new gentleness in his friend's demeanor.

One day, when he passed Brandon's work-table, Matt laid his hand on his shoulder and asked, "How's it going, Buddy?"

Brandon did not look up, but nodded, "It's good. It's good. Then he looked up. With moist eyes and asked, "But can I talk to you for minute?"

"Absolutely," Matt replied.

They sat in his office for several minutes without a word. Finally, the young man looked up. "I understand everything now and I love her more than ever. But Dr. Sheridan thinks it may be a while before she can express her love to me sexually, freely and uninhibited. And, Matt . . . well . . . I'm not sure I can be as patient and understanding as I need to be."

"Oh, my good friend," Matt said. "Let *me* tell *you* a story."

He concluded his *own* story by saying, "With God's help, you can do it. I know it. And, in the end, it will be worth your every effort."

Matt said to Brandon, "A promise. Every day, as I see you leave this office, I will stop what I'm doing and pray for you."

Chapter Twenty

Several months after Papa B retired from the company, offices were shuffled, remodeled and reconfigured. During the process, Mark, CFO, suggested that a team of officers clear out the big, walk-in safe.

"There are things piled in there that have been there as long as I can remember", he said. "Who knows? We might uncover old land-lease papers and find out we're sitting on somebody else's property?"

He, along with Breck and the company attorney undertook the project. No fortunes. No gold bricks. Mostly old papers that had been poked in there by someone who would deal with them later. Nothing. Except for a small strong-box – with a note on it.

This box contains my private papers and is not to be opened by anyone *except in the case of my demise. Taylor Harlow.* It was locked – but no key.

"It should be given to Anne to take to Taylor's mother, her only other living relative," the three concluded. Aunt Jessie had been in a nursing home for some time after suffering a stroke after Taylor's fatal accident. She would need Anne's presence, no matter what was in the box. Breck would go with her as a witness.

It held mostly personal mementos, certificates, a few pictures – but also – Taylor's *adoption* papers. Jessie uttered a weak, whispering little moan, "Oh Tay, baby."

Walter and Jessie Harlow were on vacation in the northwest big sky country a full two months before their first baby was due and it was then and there that Jessie went into labor. They were camped near a middle-sized town – large enough to have a fine hospital, but small enough to enjoy the friendliness of a rural people – both of which turned out to be a blessing. Their baby girl was stillborn.

In the same maternity ward, on the same night, a young woman came into the hospital with a basket on her arm. The night nurse noticed her and figured she was visiting and bringing a gift to a patient. The nurse turned around to answer the phone and had her back to the counter. When she completed the call, the basket still remained on the counter. She supposed the young woman had set it there while using the restroom. She thought no more about it and went on with her charting.

After a few minutes, she heard whimpering, puppy sounds from the basket. The young woman had vanished. Nurse Shaw glanced up. She listened a few seconds. A shock wave of realization soared through her. With an intensely sick feeling of dread, she knew what she would find as she carefully pulled back the towels.

Just down the hall, another tragedy, another scenario of heartbreak loomed. Walter Harlow was holding his spirit-broken wife in his arms, caressing her damp hair, pressing her against him as she sobbed. The doctor explained that, in addition to being dangerously premature, the cord was wrapped around the baby's neck and had asphyxiated her even before the emergency caesarean. As Nurse Shaw hurried to the nursery with her abandoned bundle, she encountered Dr. Logan. She opened the dirty towels and showed him. They looked at each other. A stunned Dr. Logan said to her, "Is there a chance the Lord God Almighty is working in this place?" Shaw shrugged her shoulders, but she was too overcome with emotion to answer.

Logan stood looking at the tiny unwanted infant and thought of the grieving, would-be parents he had just left.

"God, help us," he said gently.

After three days of physical examinations, psychological interviews, legal investigations, Family Services involvement, personal soul-searching, and much paper-work, Jessie and Walter Harlow took their new baby girl, Taylor Louise, home. Jessie could nurse the baby – and had been allowed to in the hospital.

Their New Baby announcements included an invitation to a Welcome Home party to see the *special souvenir* of their trip out west.

No one, but Walter and Jessie, knew the full story and they had agreed during the trip home that no one ever would. They agreed, as well, that they would not tell Taylor until she graduated from high school at eighteen, her legal age.

That explained why, at eighteen years of age, Taylor decided that since she had no identity, she was going to go for broke and show everybody. She would make her *own* identity, and herself well-known! She vowed, "I may not have the same heritage my so-called cousin has, but I'll show them all what success looks like."

Jessie admitted to Anne and Breck that they had spoiled Tay by giving her anything she wanted. "It was, I suppose, an effort to compensate. I intended to take that secret to my grave. I didn't realize Tay had kept the papers." She was devastated with worry. "Now, everyone will know."

"We will tell no one," Anne said. "Absolutely no one – except Matthew – because he and I are the same person. We share our thoughts, our griefs, our blessings. This secret, so precious to you – he will hold in total confidence and honor, as you wish. You have my word on that. And my word is his word. But," she added, "Matthew needs to know this to help him understand her."

She asked Jessie, "Would you like to destroy the paper?"

"Oh, yes."

"Tell you what. Let's go out in the yard and have a little ceremony. We'll burn this document, you sing that little lullaby you used to sing when you tucked us in at night, and we'll have a prayer."

"Oh, that's a lovely idea. That way, we can let Tay go -- and we will lock this into our memories once and for all."

Chapter Twenty-One

Claire proved to be a natural for managing The Bee Hive. Her one disappointment was that *managing* took so much of her time she didn't have enough time left for one-on-one with the children. She had a knack for evaluating potential assistants but left the final hiring to Breck's more objective experience. She found the seniors related well to the older workers and the children, and also to teens and twenty-year-olds. Probably an energy thing, she concluded. At any rate, she loved the challenge.

An interesting sidelight – there was a definite spike in applications for employment at the Breckenridge Corp – people who wanted the extra benefit of day-care for a child or parent. Anne became Claire's assistant, right-hand-man and chief bottle-washer – which, in this case, was a literal position and a precise one considering all the baby bottles. They also kept bottled water available for the older guests. Thankfully *those* bottles did not need to be washed, sanitized or warmed.

Papa B had himself driven in to help out whenever the notion struck him – he let it be known that *he was not there for day-care, he was on the steering committee, he was part owner of the building and was there to protect his investment.* He was known, on occasion, to be a bit *too* protective and had a tendency to *interfere* with management.

One day, in exasperation, Matt said, "Granddad, did it ever occur to you that there might be certain situations you are not to be in charge of?"

"Humph!"

On an antiquing spree one day, Claire noticed a set of brass knuckles from WWII. She had a sudden inspiration. "That's just what I need to have some fun," she said. The Board had been critical of her seriousness in the conduct of the operation and had been encouraging her to "Lighten up and not take things so seriously" especially on subjects over which she had little control because of government intervention and/or so-called 'social accountability' – like discipline.

At the next committee meeting, the members were shocked to see a beautiful wooden plaque prominently mounted on the wall behind the head of the table. On it was a brass plate which read, "Discipline will be maintained at all times" and mounted in the center were the brass knuckles. Underneath it was signed, "The Management".

The whole thing was so *off-the-wall* it was obviously a joke, but Claire was determined to ignore the reactions and keep a straight face.

She opened the meeting in her usual judicious way and proceeded to call for the business of the day. Some members looked at each other, some looked down at their agendas and one pretended to pick up his pen from the floor.

Finally, Papa B said, "Daughter-in-law, you are certifiable".

And the room erupted.

The Maplegove Christmas Parade was held each November, the first Saturday after Thanksgiving. This year, The Bee Hive entered a float featuring a living-room scene with a large, lighted Christmas tree. Some of the children would be sitting around the tree on homey, braided rugs or in rockers on the laps of whomever of the seniors were able and willing. Papa B was not willing. And Anne concluded that her present condition was, perhaps, a bit *too* homey.

Claire had recruited helpers who would follow along beside the float in elf suits in case one of the performers – young *or* old – decided to abandon ship. Excitement was at fever pitch as the kids received their final instructions the afternoon of the parade. They all scurried to their respective beds to take naps before time to suit up and load up.

All except four-year-old Benji Dugan – who had broken out with Chicken-Pox earlier. Benji had been quarantined within the nurse's quarters for two weeks and he was beginning to feel the isolation big time. The spots were about gone, but the self-pity still hung around. He would not be allowed to rejoin the others for another two days. He had been hearing about the parade and watching excited preparations from afar and had decided that "nothin' ain't fair." When Breck and Claire stopped by his room to tell him goodbye, he was sitting cross-legged in the middle of the floor with his little head resting on a doubled-up fist. He looked up at them while big tears streamed down his cheeks. His small shoulders sagged. He flopped his little hands into his lap and hung his head.

"I guess I'll ist stay here and sratch my itches", he said.

Claire leapt across the room and knelt before the dejected little body and gathered him in her arms.

"Oh no, darling. You must come with us. We need you." She looked at Breck with a wifely look that said, *"Do something!"*

Breck stroked his chin and said, "I think I heard the Fire Chief say they are going to be short-handed on the fire truck. They may need help. Let me call him."

The most unusual Recruitment meeting ever held at the firehouse occurred that day.

These men were often given an opportunity to volunteer for dangerous situations. They understood the risks involved, but *never* did they slack in their readiness to answer any call, any need. However, the requirements this time were simple. The chief stood before the assembled group and made the announcement. Two men were needed. Two men who had had Chicken-pox.

That was it.

Surprise registered on the team's faces. They looked questioningly up at him. Men began to smile, before the lips spread wide in jolly laughter. They figured this was the start of one of the chief's corny jokes.

He grinned. "I'm serious. What we've got here is a special little boy with Chicken-pox who very badly needs to be in the parade. We need two men in the cab of the truck, with Benji as a passenger and the official Santa watcher. I'll ride on the back with the others because I don't qualify." He looked down sheepishly and then dramatically added, "I lived a very sheltered life, you see. I missed out on the fun of Chicken-pox as a kid."

He got more volunteers than expected. He chose a couple of unmarried men who wouldn't be carrying anything home to kids of their own.

Benji wore a badge in the Christmas parade which read, BENJI DUGAN, WATCHER

Chapter Twenty-Two

The baby arrived without drama or trauma – in the middle of the night. Matt had joked to his wife, "Please don't wake me up until at least six o'clock in the morning, okay? I really don't want to be disturbed."

But about 4:00 a.m., Anne began watching the clock. Not for her husband's convenience, but to time the encroaching discomfort. At a quarter to six, she set the alarm for 6:00 a.m. and turned it to *loud*!

Later that evening, the hospital waiting room looked like a two-family reunion. Breck paused in his pacing and asked, "So who's cooking tonight, the men or the women?" He plunked down in a chair and added, "Where's Ardyth when you need her?"

In the delivery room, an exhausted Anne battled on. Matt did his best – which wasn't good enough. She grew tired of him telling her how to breathe and she was tired of the word "push" – she was just tired.

After one contraction – more succinctly known as pain – Anne looked at Matt and said, "Was this your idea or mine?" Then, "If you tell me 'You're doing fine' one more time, I'm walking out of here!" That lightened things up a bit.

Dr. Ted had come into the room – mostly to settle Matt down and to encourage Anne.

She even yelled at him, "Do something! Don't you have any scissors or anything?" "Yes, as a matter of fact, we do – but not just yet, baby. Not just yet. okay?"

After a few more deep breaths, Anne apologized, "I'm sorry. It's either *yell* or *cuss*, and I don't know how to cuss."

Dr. Ted said with a smile, "Just keep pushing, little one. It'll come to you."

The doctor in charge followed that with, "Hush. All of you. We have us a baby."

At that blessed moment, the "most beautiful baby girl ever born" slipped into the world and into the doctor's hands. Matt took one long look and slid to the floor. Dr. Ted stepped over him, looked lovingly into Anne's eyes, hugged her like a father and departed for the waiting room to announce the arrival of Elizabeth Claire Breckenridge – namesake of her grandmothers.

Afterward

People come and go through our lives and we evaluate, judge, accept or reject them by the outward signs of who and how they appear to be.

But we don't really know <u>why</u> they are who they are. Only God knows the inner heart and soul.

Each of our lives is entangled with Taylors and Ashleys and Claires and Jessies and Bubbys and Papa Bs. We weave them into the fabric of our lives – as we become a part of theirs.

When all is said and done – a worthy life is one built on faith in the Great 'I Am', hope for what is yet to come, and love for these others, whoever they are.

But the greatest of these is love.

Love -- forever -- and even beyond.

CPSIA information can be obtained
at www.ICGtesting.com
Printed in the USA
LVHW010804120119
603629LV00001B/1/P